COURTING DANGER

RUTHLESS EMPIRE

BOOK ONE

BY EVIE RILEY

SALE OF THIS BOOK WITHOUT A FRONT COVER MAY BE UNAUTHORIZED. IF THIS BOOK IS COVERLESS, IT MAY HAVE BEEN REPORTED TO THE PUBLISHER AS "UNSOLD OR DESTROYED" AND NEITHER THE AUTHOR NOR THE PUBLISHER MAY HAVE RECEIVED PAYMENT FOR IT.

NO PART OF THIS BOOK MAY BE ADAPTED, STORED, COPIED, REPRODUCED OR TRANSMITTED IN ANY FORM OR BY ANY MEANS, ELECTRONIC OR MECHANICAL, INCLUDING PHOTOCOPYING, RECORDING, OR BY ANY INFORMATION STORAGE AND RETRIEVAL SYSTEM, WITHOUT PERMISSION IN WRITING FROM THE PUBLISHER.

THANK YOU FOR RESPECTING THE HARD WORK OF THIS AUTHOR.

Courting Danger

An MM Mafia Romance

Ruthless Empire

Book One

Copyright © 2024

Evie Riley

Second Edition

ISBN: 978-1-77357-678-7

Published by Naughty Nights Press LLC

Cover Art By CDG Cover Designs

Names, characters and incidents depicted in this book are products of the author's imagination or are used fictitiously. Any resemblance to actual events, locales, organizations, or persons, living or dead, is entirely coincidental and beyond the intent of the author.

COURTING DANGER

Amidst deadly enemies and tense power struggles, the boundaries of love are put to the ultimate test.

Garrison Reyes is an ex-soldier struggling to make ends meet after retiring from the military due to a traumatic incident during his last deployment. When he is hired as a bodyguard, he sees it as an opportunity to put his combat skills to use. As Garrison becomes more entrenched in Alex's world, he realizes that his new boss is not just a wealthy businessman, but the son of the head of the Italian mafia. He sees firsthand the violence and corruption that permeates their world, and begins to question whether he can continue to work for someone involved in such a dark and dangerous organization.

Targeted by rival crime families who want to take down his father's empire, Alex Mariano is forced to take his father's position as head of the Italian mafia when his father is incarcerated. Alex is struggling with his own internal conflicts. He wants to make changes that will help the family thrive and grow stronger, but he knows that his ambitions may put him in even more danger. As tensions within the mafia empire rise, Alex finds himself in the middle of a power struggle with the last person he ever expected.

Despite their vastly different backgrounds and a significant age gap, Garrison and Alex develop a powerful attraction to each other, but their relationship is complicated by the fact that they come from opposing worlds. Garrison struggles to reconcile his feelings for Alex with his loyalty to his own moral code. Meanwhile, Alex is torn between his love for Garrison and his duty to his family and the mafia.

Can love conquer all in a world where family honor and loyalty come first? Or will they be torn apart by the very forces that brought them together?

With heart-stopping action, forbidden romance, and unexpected twists and turns, this story is a thrilling adventure that explores the boundaries of love, loyalty, and sacrifice.

CHAPTER ONE

Garrison

HOW MANY PIECES can a person lose before they're no longer themselves?

That question bounced around in my brain as I watched the woman across the room. She'd just had both her legs amputated and was learning how to use her two new prosthetics.

Half her body mass stolen in one moment. Yet, I wouldn't call her half a person. In fact, as I watched her fighting to walk again, I'd call her more a person than most.

My thoughts were interrupted when my friend Caden flopped into the seat across from me.

"I've got a great idea."

The moment those words left Caden's mouth, I immediately stood from the table. I didn't get far before he caught my sleeve.

"Come on," Caden pleaded. "It's not like the last time. I promise."

"Last time you had a *great idea*, we ended up stranded on the side of the road in Baltimore." I frowned.

"Okay, yes, that was my fault. But this is different. Just hear me out."

Running a hand through my short hair, I glanced around at the other people in the veteran hospital's therapy room. I was only there for a checkup, to make sure my knee had healed properly after being shattered by a high caliber bullet. So far everything looked good—or as good as could be expected after doctors had to literally piece my knee back together from splinters—so I felt lucky.

Many others in that room weren't so lucky. Along with the woman missing her legs, there was a man who had more bandages than visible skin, and another whose entire left side of their body seemed to be paralyzed. Even Caden had a bum leg and a barely working arm, which he was meant to be exercising.

How could I turn down a request from a friend when I was the most fortunate one in the room?

I sat back down on the cheap plastic stool that shifted under my weight. "Fine. What's this idea of yours?"

Caden propped his injured arm up on the table to keep it out of the way, then leaned forward in excitement. "Okay, so, you've been looking for work, right?"

It was obviously a rhetorical question. Caden had witnessed every step of my fruitless quest to find a job. The clock was ticking. There were only a few weeks left on the lease for my apartment. If I couldn't afford to renew the lease or move somewhere else, I'd be out on the street with no roof over my head.

Caden didn't bother to wait for my response and barreled on with his so-called *great idea*. "I work for this club, right? Just, like, courier stuff. Transporting things here and there. But, yesterday I heard the manager talking about hiring a new bouncer, so I recommended you."

The legs of the stool were uneven and

clacked like a metronome against the linoleum floor with the slightest shift in my weight. I focused on sitting as still as possible to quiet the noise and distract myself from the urge to throttle my friend.

"So, when you said you had a great idea, what you meant was that you've already made a decision and are hoping I'll just go along with it."

"Come on." Caden spread himself over the table like a half-melted ice cube. "The place is in desperate need of some decent security, and you'd be a great bouncer. Six-foot-two. Built like a brick shithouse. Natural resting-bitch-face. You'll terrify any troublemakers before they can even get started."

"Was that supposed to be a compliment or an insult?"

Cursing from the other side of the room suddenly interrupted our conversation. The woman with the prosthetic legs had collapsed. Hospital staff rushed to help her up, but she waved them away and insisted on climbing to her artificial feet on her own. She wobbled for a moment as she struggled to find her balance, but eventually stood up straight.

Looking down at my two intact legs, I flexed my right knee under the table. The joint ached more the usual today, and I felt the scar tissue pulling taut with each movement.

Yet at least I had my own feet to stand on.

I pressed my palm into the muscle above my knee, using the discomfort to ground myself. "Fine. If you've already set it up, I can at least talk to the manager. See what being a bouncer for a club would require."

"Great." With his good hand, Caden pulled out his phone and punched a few numbers. A moment later my phone buzzed with the notification of an incoming text. "Meet me at that address tomorrow night. Say... around ten. You won't regret it, I promise."

Looking up the address, I scrolled through a few pictures of the club in question. I sighed. "Too late. I already do."

CHAPTER TWO

Garrison

THE ULTRAVIOLET ROOM was... a club. I didn't have enough experience with nightclubs to judge it further than that. The lights were strobing, the music repetitive, and the average age of the people on the dance floor made me feel old.

Caden led me through the pulsing crowd toward a more secluded corner near the back. "It should be just over here. Let me see... " Mid-sentence, Caden suddenly froze, his hand smacking into my stomach to bring us both to an immediate stop. "Fuck. What's he doing here?"

Following Caden's startled gaze, I saw several people sitting around a roped off area in the corner. They were a variety of ages, but the oldest of them couldn't have been more than thirty. Based on body language, one man was obviously the de facto 'leader' of the group.

Mid-twenties, with shoulder length black hair and a smooth olive complexion, he had a youthful smile but the dark eyes of a predator.

An attractive man, my libido could easily admit that much. At first glance, he seemed like a typical upper-class rich boy, with an expensive suit tailored to fit him perfectly and an even more expensive watch sitting on his wrist. However, the silver hoop piercing his eyebrow and the pale scars crisscrossing his knuckles hinted at a dangerous edge hiding underneath the man's polished exterior.

"What's wrong? Who is that?" My voice barely carried over the volume of the club's music, but Caden heard me anyway.

"That's Alexander Mariano. Technically, he owns the club, but... I wasn't expecting him to be here. He usually stays on the other side of town."

"If he owns the club, isn't that who we should talk to?"

Shaking his head, Caden stepped back until he was completely out of Mariano's line of sight. "No, that's not... we should leave."

Since I hadn't been that committed to the idea of working for a nightclub, especially not since setting foot in the building and realizing how out of place I was in this environment, I didn't bother to protest. I turned to follow Caden, but a tickle of instinct on the back of my neck made me pause. I couldn't immediately tell what caught my attention, but a whisper inside my skull had me reaching for a gun I no longer carried.

Caden tugged at my arm. "What's up? Come on. We're leaving."

Adrenaline pumped through my veins and I felt my eyes dilate as I darted my gaze back and forth to absorb the entire scene at once. "Something's not right."

In my peripheral, I noticed Caden's expression twist with displeasure, obviously about to argue, but at the same moment I was distracted by a figure stepping out of the crowd.

A man, seemingly no different than any other patron in the club, reached inside his jacket with the slow deliberation of someone trying not to be noticed.

I reacted before my conscious mind even registered the sight of a gun.

CHAPTER THREE

Alex

ON A LIST of all the nightclubs I owned, the Ultraviolet Room wasn't my favorite. I usually preferred the Vixen. It had the perfect combination of clientele, rich and very gay.

The Ultraviolet Room, not so much.

Heaving a sigh, I downed the rest of my drink.

If I wanted to go home with someone tonight, I'd probably have to settle. The selection of partners available here was not up to my usual standard.

It had been a long day. The Mariano family may be the head of the Italian mafia, but that didn't save them from dealing with paperwork. There was so much red tape to manage and information to fabricate in order to blind the eyes of the law.

Since I refused to get involved with my family's dirtier affairs, the busy work usually fell to me. My father, David Russo, was the head of the Italian mafia, and I was the man's only child. One day that title would fall to me, but there was no reason to dive into my family's muck all at once. I preferred to wade in slowly and enjoy my freedom while I could.

After spending the day submitting fake tax forms, I hadn't felt like driving all the way across town to my preferred club. Instead, I'd headed for the nearest establishment I owned.

I was paying for that moment of laziness now by suffering through subpar company. A brunet man currently occupied my lap. The man was pretty enough, but nothing special.

From the moment I'd stepped through the door, I'd been surrounded by so-called *friends*. People just powerful enough to feel entitled to my time. I knew my bodyguard more than I knew these people, and I barely remembered the man's name. These social hyenas, I was lucky if I even remembered what family they came from.

A man sitting on the couch to my right—Harvy? Javier? —kept droning on about something to do with shipping containers. The words washed over me like white noise, and I flagged a waiter down to ask for another drink.

Eventually, a woman sitting on his left—Rachelle? Rebecca? —changed the topic to discuss the upcoming Olympics. This held my attention just long enough for me to decide I had nothing to add to the conversation. I remained silent, smiling and nodding when necessary to feign engagement. Instead, I entertained myself by imagining what I was going to do later to the brunet currently running a hand over my chest.

Maybe a good spanking before fucking him hard.

If the man wanted to act like a coquette, then I would take great pleasure bullying him to tears.

A glint of metal out of the corner of my eye suddenly caught my attention, but before I could look, someone grabbed the front of my shirt and yanked me to the floor. I landed flat on my back, knocking the air from my lungs. Then an even greater weight landed on top of me.

Half a heartbeat later, the familiar pop of a silenced gun sounded far too close for comfort.

A large body lay over me like a blanket of muscle and bone. I stared up into a stern face and gasped out a single word.

"What?"

The stranger on top of me pressed me harder into the floor, stealing what little breath I'd managed to regain.

"Stay down."

Over the stranger's shoulder, I caught the same glint of metal from before.

A gun.

Someone had just tried to shoot me. Thanks to this stranger, the bullet had missed its mark, but now the gunman was approaching to make a second attempt.

While I was still processing that fact, the stranger jumped to his feet and intercepted the gunman.

The man didn't even flinch when the weapon pointed at his face. Grabbing the gunman's wrist, he twisted the man into an arm lock and knocked the gun from his grip. Then, with a quick snap and the crunch of breaking bone, the gunman's arm hung limp.

Clutching his broken arm, the gunman shouted in surprise and pain. The noise was quickly silenced by a strike to the throat, which left the man gasping and sputtering on the ground, unable to draw breath.

Probably a collapsed windpipe, based on the blue color tinting the gunman's face. Depending on the severity of the wound, he might survive, or he might not.

I didn't care. I was too busy staring up at my savior.

Well over six feet tall, the man was built like a tank but moved like a viper. A scar sliced down his cheek, starting just under his right eye and following the strong line of his jaw like a teardrop. Overall, the man cut an intimidating figure, haloed in the neon lights of the club.

Letting my gaze trace my rescuer from head to toe, I licked my lips.

"Well, you're definitely not boring."

The man never heard me. The gunman

wasn't alone. The moment the first gunman hit the ground, another stepped out of the crowd. My savior jumped to his feet and rammed a shoulder into the gut of the nearest gunman, slamming them into the wall. The would-be assailant's head snapped back with a crack of bone against brick. He staggered but kept a grip on his gun.

A hand grabbed my arm and tried to pull me to my feet.

"Sir, we need to go."

I slapped away the hand. "There you are. About time." My bodyguard had finally joined the action, though instead of fighting off the enemy, the fucker's first instinct was to flee. I was not impressed. I'd be firing this one by the end of the night.

Another glint of steel.

My bodyguard collapsed to the floor with his throat slit from one side to the other and his life force creating a thick puddle on the floor. A third attacker, not a gunman this time, stood over the fresh corpse with a knife in one hand and a victorious smile on his face.

I sniffed in disdain. "A bit premature, don't you think? I'm not dead yet."

COURTING DANGER

Just as the word "dead" left my mouth, I kicked the knife-wielding attacker in the shin. The man hopped back, avoiding the blow, but it was enough. By then, my savior had finished with the second gunman and snuck up from behind to wrap an arm around the third attacker's throat.

Struggling to get free, the attacker tried stabbing my rescuer with the butt of the knife. He caught the man's flailing wrist in one hand, twisting it until the asshole dropped the weapon. Unarmed, the assailant could only flail as the arm around his throat squeezed until he passed out.

Four bodies lay sprawled over the floor, one dead and three unconscious. My champion stood over them, his expression just as serious and restrained as he had been with a gun pointed at his head. There was no victory in this man's eyes, only an intense focus. Like a knife that refused to be sheathed, he was ready for the next fight.

Actually, there were five bodies on the floor.

I realized with disgust that I'd spent the entire fight lying on the ground like a damned swooning maiden. Quickly getting to my feet, I dusted myself off and then turned to face my knight in shining armor.

What exactly did one say in a situation like this?

It wasn't my first fight, not by a long shot. It was, however, the first time I'd been rescued by a complete stranger. Simply saying "thank you" seemed too cheap.

Should I offer compensation?

No. That might make it look like I was trying to get rid of the man as quickly as possible.

Quite the opposite.

I really wanted to drag this man home with me.

Before I had the chance to say anything, however, the ringing of my phone interrupted my musing. Resisting the urge to snarl in frustration, I brought the phone to my ear without looking at the identity of the caller. Only a few people had my personal number.

"You'd better have some answers, because someone just tried to kill me."

To my shock, my mother's familiar voice greeted me from the other end of the line.

"Alex, you need to come home."

Her words were smooth and unhurried. To anyone else she would have sounded relaxed. I knew better. Her accent was heavier than normal, indicating how much effort she was putting into maintaining her calm facade.

I gripped the phone in both hands. "Mother? What's going on? Did you hear what I just said?"

"I heard. Our enemies are moving even faster than I feared."

"What are you talking about? Why would anyone suddenly try to kill a member of our family? That's basically suicide."

"Your father... " My mother's voice wavered in a moment of uncharacteristic emotion. "Your father's been arrested."

CHAPTER FOUR

Alex

A FEW HOURS later, I found myself sitting at the end of a long table facing my mother. The Mariano family owned over a dozen houses in almost as many countries, so there was no one location that I considered *home*. When my mother requested that I come home, what she actually meant was to meet her wherever she was at the time. At first, I'd feared that meant traveling to our house in Venice where she usually preferred to stay during the spring. Luckily, she had already flown into our Matoloking residence, so I only had to travel an hour and a half from Newark.

Serafina Mariano was a petite woman with the look of a strict schoolteacher. Her dark hair was pulled into a tight bun without a single hair out of place. Despite being over forty, she showed not a hint of gray, though I couldn't be certain if it was a result of good genetics or hair dye.

I sat in a high-backed chair, one leg crossed over the other and my chin braced on my fist. There were three other people seated at intervals down one side of the table, but I ignored them for now and kept my attention on my mother at the far end.

"So, how exactly did father get himself arrested on human trafficking charges when he's already in prison?"

The Matoloking house, like most of the Mariano homes, was a mix of antique and modern design. This meant a lot of clean lines and open spaces, complemented with older details around the edges. My voice echoed just a little too much for comfort, though not enough to be truly uncomfortable.

At the other end of the table, my mother shifted position so her fingers intersected like a steeple, allowing her to peer over them and create the illusion that she was bigger than she actually was. "I'm wondering about that myself, but I've held off on this conversation until you were here." She glanced over her shoulder at the man standing adjacent to her chair. "Valente? Surely you have an answer."

Valente Guerra. Bodyguard, gopher, and all around right-hand-man to my father. He reminded me of a panther, dressed in a deceptively simple black suit that easily concealed half a dozen weapons. In his entire life, I couldn't remember once seeing my father without Valente just a step behind.

Looking at the man now, standing alone in the vast room, he looked like half a person.

Tipping his head in a slight bow, Valente addressed the room in general as though speaking to a crowd.

"The Boss was out on a day pass and we were conducting an inspection of one of our facilities in Baltimore. We'd received reports where the numbers didn't add up. Product going missing. Delayed payments. That sort of thing. Unfortunately, during the inspection, local police conducted a raid of the facility. The Boss was caught on location and arrested. That, alone, we could have handled, but it turned out that some of the products were minors from other countries, which drew the attention of Interpol."

I tapped the toe of my polished shoe against the leg of the table, a staccato of irritation that matched the twitching of my eyebrow. "On a day pass... It turned out... " I repeated, putting just enough emphasis on the words to make my mockery of Valente's words clear.

"You say that like my father didn't know he was trafficking literal children. He couldn't even wait till he'd gotten out, for fuck's sake? He only had a few months left! I hope you aren't foolish enough to think this whole thing was a coincidence." I rolled my eyes, knowing my disrespect would piss the man off. I didn't care.

This time it was my mother who responded, snorting daintily through her nose and waving one hand in the air like batting away a fly. "Of course not. The police showing up right when your father was visiting is too coincidental. It was obviously a setup. At first, we thought it was only an attack against your father, someone trying to take him out of the game permanently, but now that someone's made an attempt on your life, it seems they're after the entire Mariano family. Until we figure out who is behind this attack, we all have to be extra careful."

For the first time, I paid attention to the three people seated along the side of the table. Bloody and bruised, one of them was barely conscious, kept upright only by the ropes binding him to the chair. Another bled profusely from both ears, likely the result of punctured eardrums, and sobbed quietly to himself through a gag. Only the third person, seated closest to me, remained fully cognizant. He said nothing and barely moved as he glared daggers at me, his teeth grinding against the gag and his hands repeatedly flexing into fists.

The three had been in much better condition when they'd been trying to kill me. No doubt their new wounds were a result of Valente's work.

I gestured toward the bound captives. "You've already questioned the people who attacked me. If you still don't know who's behind it, then I assume they were hired anonymously."

My mother nodded, barely sparing the three a glance. "It was a careful job. No names. They never met the person who hired them, and all communication was made through a burner phone. Our only hope right now is to track down the store where the phone was purchased and get access to their security cameras. It'll take some time, and there's no telling how long the case against your father could drag on. Right now, the family needs a strong leader. It's time for you to step into your responsibilities as the Mariano heir. If your father is released, then he can resume his position, but until then, you are now the acting head of this family."

I dropped my casual posture, leaning forward with my elbows on the table in a way that would have earned me a cane to the knuckles when I was younger. "What? Why am I suddenly in charge? Why not you? You've got more experience."

A slight pause before answering was the only indication of my mother's irritation "Experience doesn't matter as much as blood. I married into the Russo family, I'm also a woman, and as such, I will never command as much respect as someone, a male, born with both Russo and Mariano blood. It has to be you, or we risk looking weak to the other families."

I recognized my mother's stubborn expression. It looked almost the same as all her other expressions—the woman had a legendary poker face—except an extra tightness pinched the corners of her mouth.

There would be no arguing with her. If I tried, it would be the same as bashing my head against a wall. Painful and ultimately pointless.

"Fine. I'll take over as head of the family… for now. So, if you'll excuse me, it's late and I apparently need to get ready for a very busy day tomorrow."

I stood with as much decorum as I could muster, breathing a silent sigh of relief when neither my mother nor Valente called me back. On my way out of the room, I stopped just behind the seat of the attacker who had been glaring at me. Pulling out a thin silver knife from the inner pocket of my jacket, I fisted a hand in the man's hair and plunged the knife into his eye.

My attacker writhed against his bonds,

screaming through the gag, but I just held on tighter as I twisted the knife. I was careful not to let the blade slip too deep. After all, I didn't want to puncture the brain and accidentally kill my assailant. The man still had plenty of uses. I just couldn't stand the arrogance in the man's eyes. Even beaten and bound, the man still had the audacity to glare at me. Fucker.

Satisfied that the offending eye had been permanently dealt with, I removed my knife and released the man, letting him slump against his ropes. Then, giving my mother and Valente a nod, I left them all behind.

Like everything else in a Mariano house, the hallways of this particular residence were large and grand, giving me plenty of time to think as I hiked to the front door. Using a silk handkerchief stored in my pocket, I absentmindedly and methodically cleaned the blood from my knife as I reviewed the last twelve hours. When I woke up this morning, my biggest concern had been boredom. Now, I was burdened by too much excitement, and not the kind I enjoyed.

Tossing the stained handkerchief into

a trashcan, I heaved a sigh. "I need a drink."

"You're not taking this seriously."

Stopping in the middle of the hall, I turned toward the sound of the familiar voice. My cousin sat half hidden on a window bench. She held a book in her hands that was open to a page somewhere in the middle, as if she'd been lounging there for hours.

I wasn't fooled.

"Long time no see, Ghita. Eavesdropping on people's conversations is rude, you know."

Ghita had inherited the short stature of most Mariano women, but with the added benefit of more curves. She also kept her dark hair in a modernly short, asymmetrical cut that made the traditional members of our family click their tongues in disapproval.

She set her book aside, not bothering to mark her page as she gave up the innocent act.

"I don't need to eavesdrop. It's obvious just from the look on your face. You aren't taking this threat seriously. Someone tried to kill you tonight, and they're certainly going to try the same thing with your father."

Despite being a year older than me, when Ghita stood she only reached the center of my chest. I ruffled her hair in the way I knew she hated, just to see her pout.

"This isn't the first time Father's ended up on the wrong side of the law. It's an occupational hazard in this family, but he always manages to wriggle his way out, in the end. Just you wait. In a few weeks the charges will be dropped, he'll be out of jail again, and everything will return to status quo. Besides... " In my hand I still held the recently cleaned knife. I twirled it between my fingers like a butterfly darting between flower petals. "I'm not exactly helpless."

With quick, precise movements, Ghita plucked the knife from my grip and tossed it over her shoulder. The sharp blade planted point first in the wall. "Still, I'd feel better if I knew you were taking this seriously. At least get some extra security in case you're attacked again."

Bits of drywall floated to the floor when I retrieved my knife. "Fine. I need a new bodyguard anyway. But this time I'm choosing them myself. The last one was a major disappointment."

I could tell my cousin still wasn't happy, but she seemed to realize further arguing would be pointless and let the matter drop.

"Fine. Better than nothing. But if you get killed, I swear I won't grieve at your funeral."

Just for my own amusement, I ruffled her hair again. "Sure you won't. I'll see you later, GeeGee."

She gnashed her teeth at me as she smoothed her hair back into place. It was a good sign for me to leave before I lost a hand.

A few dozen yards away, the hall opened into the front foyer. Here, I stopped and looked up at the large painting that hung above the door. It showed me when I was younger, standing beside my father who sat on a wingback chair. My mother was positioned just behind us, one hand on her husband's shoulder. Although created only fifteen years ago when I was ten, it was styled to look like an antique oil painting.

Everything about the image was fake.

They never even posed for the picture. It had been computer generated. If they had posed for it, they would have needed to glue me to the floor to get me to sit still long enough, and my mother would have had to stand on a box to be seen over the tall chair. Not to mention my father would have had to actually be present, instead of serving the first of his many stints in prison for the murder of a New Jersey couple. How the man always managed to get caught red-handed, I'd never know. My grandfather would probably roll over in his grave if he knew his legacy had turned into this kind of circus.

Since its creation, I had barely given the painting a second thought, but I stared up at it now, meeting the gaze of my father's recreated eyes. I'd never noticed before, but they were the same shape and color as my own.

David Russo was a complicated man, to say the least. Marrying my mother and combining the Russo family with the Mariano family, their biggest rivals at the time, made him the most powerful man in the mafia at a very young age. Maintaining his position at the very top of the Italian crime syndicate from the time he was thirty was not a simple feat, but by force and by loyalty to the original families, he managed to uphold the legacy he'd been given. Well, the thrill of the power he held over others went to his head and he started making stupid mistakes rather quickly. My father held a lot of traditional beliefs that probably contributed to his multiple arrests, including insisting on checking the problematic facilities in their portfolio himself to show his willingness to get his hands dirty.

A little too dirty.

I didn't know what to think about my father sitting in prison through most of my childhood and my formative teenage years. My father had been a hard man to live under, but he had his soft moments as well. Somehow he'd managed to maintain his business, keep his wife's family in line, and be somewhat of a father to me despite his on again, off again incarceration. For many years, I'd looked up to him, my silver-haired idol, and wanted to be just like him.

Now, at twenty-five, I knew better.

Two years ago, an engagement had been arranged for me with a girl from one of our rival families. It had been meant as a way to forge alliances and was exactly the same way my own parents had ended up married.

Rather than follow tradition, I had taken that opportunity to come out as gay, insisting I could never make any bride happy. I'd expected punishment, reprimand, maybe even disownment.

What I hadn't expected was for my father, after a long moment of silent contemplation, to sigh and reach for the nearby phone.

"I guess I should tell the Vidales family that the engagement is off."

For all his traditional values, my aging father had simply accepted my declaration and moved on to the day's business as if nothing untoward even happened. I had to respect the man for that, considering I knew it had to go against every ingrained thought my father had ever had. It wasn't what he'd been taught as "acceptable" but he accepted it anyway. In his own way, my father loved me, his only legitimate son, and he would do what he had to to make sure I was happy.

From that moment on, I had been free to live openly, at least as far as my sexuality was concerned. I would never call my father a *good* man, but in this one instance he'd been exactly the supportive parent that I needed.

Now it was my father who needed support, and I was going to try, even if I thought the whole thing unnecessary. Just as I'd told Ghita, my father would likely be out of prison before I was even officially recognized as the head of the family.

A sleek black car waited for me right in the middle of the house's long turnaround driveway. The engine was already running, just waiting for me to slip inside. I practically collapsed against the backseat, directing the driver to my Newark apartment as my mind buzzed with all the things I'd need to take care of tomorrow. It was going to be a nightmare, and now I had to hire a bodyguard on top of everything because I refused to break a promise to my cousin.

An idea came to me, lighting up inside my brain like a candle glowing at the center of a hurricane.

Pulling out my phone, I dialed one of the few numbers saved in my contact list.

"Hey, Ricco. Get me the footage from the Ultraviolet Room's security cameras.

Yes, from tonight. There's something I want to look into."

CHAPTER FIVE

Garrison

THE SUN WAS barely peeking over the tops of the trees as I reached the end of my fourth mile. I began most mornings with a run through the nearby park, always ending at exactly the same time. However, this morning I'd gotten a late start. The previous evening had been unexpectedly hectic, first fighting off a murder attempt, and then spending several hours being questioned by police.

They hadn't even seemed to care about my answers, just filling out the paperwork so they could file the whole thing away.

This resulted in not getting home until

the early hours of the morning, which threw off my sleep schedule and caused me to wake up late.

As I started the fifth mile, I checked my watch.

Still four and a half minutes behind.

I needed to run faster if I wanted to get my routine back on schedule.

I sucked in a deep break, my lungs filling with brisk morning air, and relished the burn of my muscles as I started running faster.

By the time I finished the park's six-mile loop, I was exactly on schedule. My right knee throbbed with each step, but the dull ache was easy enough to ignore.

So far, it was a good day.

My usual path ended near the park's playground. It took me exactly one minute and twenty-eight seconds to pass by the area. The playlist I listened to while running had been curated so the last song ended just as I reached my car. I removed the earbuds and reached for the door handle, barely noticing the sounds around me.

Before I could open the door, however, a child screamed.

My heart rate immediately jumped,

and I spun to press my back against the side of the car. My gaze darted around for the threat while I grasped in my waistband for a gun that wasn't there.

The scream turned into loud sobbing. I tracked the sound to its source, finding a toddler-aged boy sitting on the ground under the slide. His tiny fists were balled up and pressing against the boy's eyes as he cried.

A moment later, the boy's mother picked him up out of the mulch and brushed him off, calming his tears with the efficiency of an experienced parent.

I breathed a sigh of relief when the noise ended, only then peeling myself away from the side of my car and opening the door. As I slid inside, I shook my head in frustration. Adults could make any noise they wanted and I wouldn't care, but the sound of a child screaming sent me jumping like a jackrabbit.

Before I started driving, I took a moment to cycle through a few breathing exercises. May as well make use of the only thing I'd gotten out of my mandated therapy.

After a minute, I was calm enough to maneuver my car onto the street, but pain throbbed in my knee like a second heartbeat, and my scars felt stiffer than before.

Maybe today wasn't so good after all.

The ringing of my phone while I was parked at a red light emphasized that thought. Someone was calling me rather than just texting, which meant it must be serious. I answered the phone, stopping just long enough to check the caller's identity.

"Caden? What's wrong? Something about last night?"

Caden's voice sounded weak over the connection, so much so that I checked the volume on my phone.

"Garrison, hey, um, sort of. I just received a strange request. Look, I'm not the best person to explain this. I've just sent you an address. How soon can you get there?"

"I'm in the car right now, so about ten minutes. Why? What's going on?"

"Good. Go there right away. He can explain it to you."

The light turned green, but my foot stayed planted on the break.

"*He* who? What are you talking about?"

The phone beeped and fell silent.
"Caden? *He* who?"

CHAPTER SIX

Garrison

THE ADDRESS TURNED out to be a high-end tailor. I stared at the scrolling gilded letters over the entrance, comparing the address to the numbers on my phone several times before I felt confident enough to step inside. A bell chimed above the door, announcing my presence to an empty room.

Dark wood paneling acted as a backdrop to the suits displayed along the walls. Just looking at the expensive fabric made me hyper-aware of the fact I was still in my running sweats.

"You got here quicker than I thought."

The man I had saved last night stood framed in a doorway at the back of the room. Today, he was dressed more casually in dark jeans and a black button-down shirt. The top few buttons were undone, and the sleeves were rolled up to reveal his forearms. Yet, even dressed down, there was still a polish to him that fit right in with the rich ambiance of the store.

Before I could decide what question to ask first—I had a lot—the man turned around and stepped out of sight.

"Over here. We've got the place to ourselves, but I assume you'll want some privacy."

The man was so confident that his command would be followed that I had no choice but to comply. A short hallway lay beyond the main room, lined on either side by several doors. One stood open in invitation, revealing a moderately sized room with a single couch and a round pedestal in front of a wall of mirrors.

I froze in the doorway. "I'm sorry. Who are you?"

Propping one hip against the arm of the couch, the man pouted as if upset, but his dark eyes glinted with humor.

"Aw. I'm hurt, you don't remember me."

Still eyeing the man warily, I took one step through the doorway into the light from the chandelier hanging above. I was certain Caden had said the man's name at some point last night, but in all the chaos I had forgotten.

"I remember you, but we've never been introduced. Who are you?"

The man stuck out his hand. "Alexander Mariano. Alex." He paused for a moment, an expectant air hanging over his shoulders as he waited to see what I would do.

Not knowing what else Alex expected, I shook his hand. Alex wore several rings, and the metal created points of cold contact in the otherwise warm handshake.

Before I could also introduce myself, Alex turned away and took a sprawling seat on the couch.

"No need to ask who you are. Garrison Reyes. Forty-two. Unmarried. No children. No siblings. Parents moved to the west coast years ago. Former Army Ranger. Served in the military for almost twenty years and reached the level of Sergeant Major before injury forced you to retire.

Involved in quite a few black ops missions, especially in the later years of your service. Your files have more redacted spaces than actual words. Very impressive." He rattled off the information with the ease of reading from a list.

I took a step back until I was almost out of the room again. "You know a lot about me after just meeting last night."

Alex's laughter rose into the air and tangled with the jewels of the chandelier. "Of course. You can find almost anything about someone if you know where to look. The only thing about you I couldn't find was your measurements. Seriously, have you never gotten a single suit tailored before?" His gaze flickered over me from head to toe, lingering for a moment at waist level. "Not that this look doesn't suit you, but as my bodyguard you'll need to maintain a certain level of professionalism. So..." He gestured toward the pedestal.

Not one to be pushed around, I stayed by the door, crossing my arms over my chest in a stance of defiance. "Your bodyguard? Is that what this is about? I don't remember agreeing to such a thing."

I'd considered pursuing employment

as a bodyguard, but security agencies required a license I didn't have, and my financial issues needed a more immediate solution. Plus, it was only a month ago that I'd finally started walking without a noticeable limp.

Alex waved away my concern. "I didn't ask, and I'm not asking now. Asking gives people the option to say no, and I don't like being denied. After last night, it's obvious you have the skills, and as you saw, I'm in need of protection. So, I've decided, you're going to be my bodyguard."

Carefully watching Alex's body language with my peripheral, I met the other man's gaze. "And if I say no?"

Instead of growing tense, as I expected, Alex's posture relaxed slightly. "Why would you? Your debts are racking up after being injured on your last mission a year ago. Those military benefits did not go far enough, did they? I'm offering you a salary that could solve all your problems, and all you need to do is follow me around and make sure I don't die. If you still insist on rejecting the job. Well... " He shrugged casually, spinning one of his rings on his finger. "You're about two weeks from ending up on the street. Maybe you'll find another job in that time... or maybe you won't."

Light from the chandelier danced in Alex's eyes, illuminating shades of green within the black. It reminded me of the iridescence of a scarab's shell.

This was a test.

Alex was being difficult on purpose to see how I would react. The man had the personality of a trickster god, pushing buttons and challenging boundaries just for the fun of a little chaos.

Well, I had plenty of experience answering challenges.

With slow but deliberate steps, I approached the couch. My height allowed me to tower over Alex's seated position as I stood just in front of the other man.

A heated moment of silence passed between us.

Both of Alex's arms were draped over the back of the couch and his knees spread just a little too much. It was an oddly vulnerable position that invited my eyes to wander.

And wander they did.

I couldn't help noticing the way the man's tight jeans emphasized his narrow waist and lean legs.

I caught a glimpse of my own reflection in the wall-sized mirror. The hint of gray at my temples reminded me of our age difference.

If only I were ten years younger.

Alex couldn't be more than twenty-five. A man that age wouldn't have any serious interest in someone seventeen years his senior. He probably had a harem of barely legal beauties eager to climb into his bed.

Knowing the other man wasn't serious with this teasing actually made it easier for me to play along. I'd always struggled with flirting, afraid to say the wrong thing and turn my partner off. Now, however, there was no pressure. I couldn't disappoint a partner who wasn't serious in the first place, so it wouldn't matter if I made a fool of myself.

Squaring my shoulders, I used every inch of my height to my advantage and smirked as I stared down at Alex. "You're a manipulative little shit, aren't you."

It was subtle, but for a brief moment Alex shifted forward like a child eagerly expecting a present. Then he seemed to catch himself and relaxed back into the sofa, tucking a stray lock of hair behind his ear.

"I know how to get what I want. And I want you as my bodyguard. So, get on the pedestal. You need some proper clothing if you're going to be following me around."

I cast the pedestal and its wall of mirrors a considering look. Stepping onto that little disk would be the same as agreeing to Alex's demands.

"All right, I'll do what you want if you answer one question." This time Alex didn't respond, just tipped his head in a brief nod for me to continue. "Why do you need protection?"

It was almost anticlimactic how easily Alex answered, giving a brief explanation of how his father was a businessman who'd gotten in trouble with the law and made a lot of enemies. Now Alex needed to take over the family business, but his father's enemies were targeting him.

The explanation was so straightforward that it left me unsatisfied. I expected something more deserving of the promise I'd offered to earn the information. Still, we'd made a deal, so once Alex reached the end of the disappointing tale, I nodded and stepped onto the pedestal.

COURTING DANGER

As soon as my foot touched the raised circle, another older gentleman stepped through the door. I didn't even have time to ask about the stranger's identity before the man pulled out a tape measure.

Ah, a tailor. Probably employed by the shop.

Had the man been waiting just out of sight for Alex's signal?

I wasn't sure if I was alarmed or impressed by such a level of efficiency.

The tailor, apparently named Raymond based on the name stitched onto his uniform, gestured to a side table by the wall of mirrors. "You can put your clothes here, sir."

I clutched the front of my sweatshirt as if it would be yanked off me. "Is that really necessary?"

The tape measure hung coiled around Raymond's hands like a domesticated snake. "The measurements will be more accurate without clothing in the way. I can't allow you to walk about in an ill-fitting suit. It would ruin our store's reputation." Raymond spoke with gentle, measured words, but he would obviously not be dissuaded.

Sighing in resignation, I started to pull

off my sweatshirt but hadn't uncovered more than an inch of my stomach before I remembered my audience. Smoothing my shirt back into place, I raised an eyebrow at Alex.

"Do you mind? A little privacy would be nice."

Sometime during the exchange with Raymond, Alex had procured a glass of wine. The red liquid swirled as Alex continued to watch him. "I'm not going to miss a free show."

He sipped his wine, never breaking eye contact as he waited to see what I would do.

Another test.

I suspected this would be a common occurrence while working for Alex. The man may act unconcerned, but an obvious vein of distrust ran deep through his soul. Alex was prodding me, seeing what it would take to get me to react.

If I wanted to win my new employer's trust, I was going to have to match Alex at the man's own game.

Grabbing the bottom hem of my sweatshirt, I ripped the article of clothing over my head. "It's hardly free when you're paying me."

COURTING DANGER

That reminded me, Alex had mentioned a salary, but not given any specific numbers. Before I could truly call myself the man's bodyguard, we would need to hash out the details of my employment.

Taking another sip from his wine, Alex crossed one leg over the other and settled more comfortably into the couch. "Well, then I'm definitely not going to miss a show I'm paying for."

The rest of my clothes found a home on the side table, each neatly folded before they were stored. I stood on the pedestal in just my underwear and knee brace, forcing myself not to shiver in the air conditioning as Raymond began measuring.

When would the questions start?

It was inevitable whenever someone saw me shirtless for the first time. My flesh was a complicated map of scars, charting the path of my service one injury at a time. The extensive burns on my back always earned the most questions. Still fresh and pink with new healing, they stood out more than any other mark on my skin.

The proverbial 'X' on my map that

marked the end of my military career.

Yet, the expected questions never came. In fact, Alex said nothing as he watched me being measured. Then, when Raymond brought out sample suits for me to try on, Alex's only comments were about fabric choice and color preference.

By the time we finished with the tailor, nearly three hours had passed. A basic black suit had been purchased that was close enough to my measurements for me to wear immediately. It was a little loose in the waist in order to fit the width of my chest and shoulders, but I'd been assured that the rest of the ordered clothing would be custom tailored to my size.

For my own peace of mind, I didn't ask about the price.

After everything was settled, Alex dragged me outside the shop into the backseat of a car already waiting for us. Apparently, when Alex said he wanted to hire me as a bodyguard, he meant right away. As the car pulled away from the curb, Alex thrust a tablet into my hands. On the screen was a contract spelling out the details of employment. It was a generous offer, with an even more generous salary.

COURTING DANGER

I carefully picked through every word of the contract. I didn't even notice the city passing outside the car window as I squinted over the fine print. Everything seemed in order. The only oddity that caught my attention was the confidentiality clause. It took up a significant portion of the contract and reminded me of being initiated into the Special Forces again.

Suspicious, but not necessarily a deal breaker.

I knew the importance of secrecy, and I didn't care about whatever skeletons were hidden in the Mariano family's closet. I'd kept so many secrets in my life thanks to my previous job and I had no interest in digging up more.

By the time the car reached its destination, I had signed the contract. Perhaps it was too quick. Perhaps I should have gotten a second opinion before offering up my name.

But what choice did I have?

I needed the money, and I wasn't going to get a better job offer in the next two weeks.

Even if everything went wrong, what did I have to lose?

My life?

I'd already risked that so many times it had no value left.

As Alex took the tablet back, one of the man's hands came to rest just above my knee. It could have almost been mistaken for an accident, except for the way Alex squeezed the muscles of my thigh. Alex said nothing, and I didn't tell him to stop. We both pretended the hand was completely innocent, even as it crept another inch higher.

We were interrupted when the driver opened the door, silently indicating it was time for us to leave. Alex cleared his throat, then stored the tablet away in one of the car's compartments.

"After you." He gestured for me to get out first. "You've got to make sure everything's safe for me, right?"

"That would be a lot easier if I knew what we were doing."

"Meeting with my uncle." Once we were out of the car, Alex clung to my arm and pouted up at me like the heroine of a horror film begging her boyfriend to go investigate the weird noise in the basement. "You have to protect me. Uncle Lorenz isn't happy about me taking over the business. For all I know, he's behind the recent attempt on my life."

This gave me pause. "Do you really think your own family could be the ones threatening you?"

Alex laughed and dropped the helpless maiden act, but there was no hesitation before he answered. "Absolutely. My family would slit anyone's throat, even one of our own, if it meant securing a little more power."

How could he say such a thing so casually?

I had never been particularly close to the few family members I had left, but I would still balk at the idea of any of them trying to kill me. Yet Alex treated it as a common annoyance, like students cheating off each other in school. I didn't know the man well enough to tell if the nonchalance was a facade, or if Alex truly didn't care about familicide.

A red brick courtyard led to the front doors of The New Jersey Performing Arts Center. I had passed by the modern construction many times before, but never set foot inside. The building played with contrasts. Made out of brick and glass, the harsh materials were given a veneer of softness through the use of curved lines.

Just inside the front doors, another man approached them. My hackles rose as I tracked the man's movements. Even when Alex greeted the man—apparently named Valente—I didn't lower my defenses. We had just established that family could also be enemies. I hadn't been given a gun, or any sort of weapon yet. If I needed to protect Alex, the situation would get messy.

"Who's this?" Valente said in lieu of returning Alex's greeting.

Alex patted my arm. "This is my new bodyguard? What'd you think?"

Valente looked me up and down, eyes narrowing in suspicion. "We already have plenty of bodyguards on staff. There was no reason to bring in someone new."

It only took one look at Valente's stance for me to recognize a fellow warrior. The man was older than me, but not by much. Maybe late fifties at most. We both had gray in our hair. It was only a matter of ratio. My dark hair showed a little gray at the temples, while most of Valente's color had vanished.

Ignoring the obvious tension, Alex

continued forward, forcing both me and Valente to trail behind him. "Yeah, but those are your people. I wanted one of my own. Now, I need to speak with Uncle Lorenz. Is he already inside?"

The building's contrast of hard and soft continued into the main theater area. Harsh red and gold were softened by arching lines, and the whole audience was seated in a curve around the stage. Crescent-moon layers stacked on top of each other to form walls of private viewing booths that loomed over the common seats.

We found a man sitting alone in a booth on the highest levels of the theater. His swarthy coloring and handsome features easily marked him as a member of Alex's family.

It seemed innocent, and I almost relaxed, until I looked toward the stage. Of all the things I expected to find, a teen beauty pageant hadn't even been on the list. I could only think of a few reasons for a middle-aged man to be watching a pageant of literal children, alone, in a private booth. Every single option churned my stomach.

Alex must have noticed my reaction,

for he pulled us both to the other side of the hall. "Welcome to my uncle's version of a strip club. Disgusting, I know, but there's no law dictating how a person can enjoy a public event."

As much as I wanted to shout, I kept my voice down and whispered so my words wouldn't reach inside the private booth. "Shouldn't you warn the event staff? What if he tries to approach one of the girls?"

"We have warned them, but my uncle funds the scholarships that they award to the contestants, so they're not going to kick him out. I'm just telling you not to worry. I've got... eyes on him."

Looking back through the door, I saw Valente approach Alex's uncle, bending over to whisper something in the man's ear. I didn't trust either of them, but at least Valente was keeping Alex's uncle distracted. Every moment that man wasn't looking at the stage full of brightly dressed girls was a moment I could breathe.

"Is it wrong of me to hope that your uncle is the one who tried to kill you, so the police have an excuse to arrest him?"

Alex's laughter drew everyone's

attention, including several people in the adjacent booths. He stopped only when he noticed Valente and his uncle looking at him, then leaned up to whisper directly into my ear. "If he is the one trying to kill me, he won't live long enough to be arrested." Then he laughed again.

Was that meant to be a joke?

Or was Alex truly entertained by the thought of killing his own uncle?

Either way, in this instance, I found I really didn't care.

Inside the private booth, Alex slid into the seat next to his uncle while I found a position guarding the door. It allowed me to watch the hallway outside, while also keeping an eye on the predator inside.

Nephew and uncle sat in silence, watching the pageant. Time ticked by with neither speaking as several more contestants paraded across the stage. I refused to check my watch, such fidgeting would look unprofessional, but at least twenty minutes must have passed in that same way. It was the quietest and most uncomfortable battle of wills I had ever witnessed.

The pageant announced that they were moving on to the swimsuit portion of the competition when Alex's uncle finally broke the silence and sighed. "Alex. Whatever you're here for, just get it over with."

Having won the standoff, Alex sounded too happy for the situation when he replied. I couldn't see either of their expressions since I was standing behind the pair, but I could already picture the way Alex's eyes would glint in the colorful stage lights.

"I assume you've heard about my father's predicament."

"And your recent promotion. Yes. What about it?"

"I just wanted to check in. Make sure we're on the same page."

Alex's uncle turned to face his nephew, giving me a clear look at his profile. The stage lights created a white line around the edge of his face, making him look like a paper cutout of a person that had been glued onto the scene. "I'm on the same page I've always been on. The well-being of this family is my first concern, no matter who claims to be in charge."

A bright flash of light cut through the shadowed atmosphere as Alex showed his uncle something on his phone. "That's funny, because I distinctly remember my father deciding to end our collaboration with the Vidales family in the northern warehouse. So, what were you doing there? Did you think, in the chaos of everything happening, I wouldn't notice. Or did you assume you'd be the one to replace my father and went ahead with your own plans?"

Growling low under his breath, Alex's uncle knocked the phone away. "That deal with the Vidales would be beneficial for all of us. David only called it off because he's a coward. It's no surprise he raised a fag son. You're even more gutless than your father."

Standing guard on the other side of the door, I noticed Valente growing tense.

Did the man have an issue with the disrespectful tone, or the reference to Alex's sexuality?

I really wanted a gun right now. Although I wouldn't use it in this situation, the weight of a holster on my hip would have provided some stability.

Clicking his tongue like a disappointed schoolteacher, Alex stood and stored his phone back in his pocket. "You can throw around all the insults you want. It doesn't change which of us is in charge. Now, stop whatever you're doing with the Vidales family, and I'll forget this whole thing ever happened."

As Alex turned to leave, his uncle called after him. "Boy, you clearly don't know what you're doing. This isn't how you make allies."

With one hand on the doorframe, standing half in the light of the hall, Alex smiled back at his uncle. "If it's true that our family's well-being is your first concern, then I shouldn't have to make you an ally. You should already be one. If you aren't an ally, then... what are you?"

No response, and Alex didn't wait around for one. He left without a second look back. The swimsuit competition was over, and thanks to Alex's distraction, the other man had missed everything.

I hid my inner smile behind a stoic expression as I followed Alex outside.

Once again, a car was already waiting for us. Right before stepping inside, Alex stopped to issue one final order.

"Oh, Valente. Since he's my bodyguard now, Garrison needs some proper weapons. Take care of that."

Valente's eyes narrowed at me and his

teeth ground against each other. "Of course."

Such obvious hatred couldn't be ignored. It was going to cause a problem sooner or later, but I didn't have time to worry as Alex pulled me into the car.

The door closed behind us, and we were alone again.

CHAPTER SEVEN

Alex

I WAS SILENT for most of the car ride. My expression remained impassive, but my hand gripped tight to the handle of the knife in my pocket. Luckily Garrison seemed to sense the tension and watched the view beyond the window without a word.

Closing my eyes, I counted my breaths.

One, two, three.
Inhale.
One, two, three.
Exhale.
This lasted for most of the car ride.

When we turned onto the street of our destination, I flexed my hand against the pins-and-needles feeling running under my skin. I'd been gripping the knife handle so hard that my fingers had gone numb, and my knuckles were sore from grinding together.

The car rolled to a stop in front of a building made of tan stone. Time and weather had turned the copper adornments into an appealing shade of green. Most of the building's body sat as a long low rectangle, but a tall section in the middle with a domed ceiling gave it some height.

As I stepped out of the car, I kept an eye on Garrison. I almost never brought anyone home with me, but when I did there were always interesting reactions.

Garrison did not disappoint.

"A police station?" The man's face barely moved, but that only made the slight twitches in his expression even more telling. It was a fascinating dance of subtlety.

Too bad I couldn't enjoy the show properly. I ignored the security guards standing to either side of the front doors as I stormed past and spoke to Garrison over my shoulder.

"Not anymore. The station shut down decades ago and the building was abandoned. Three years ago, I bought it and turned it into apartments. Such beautiful antique architecture shouldn't be left to rot."

Inside the building's front lobby of white marble and black carpet, I paused to look back at the security guards by the door. One of them was speaking into their phone.

Sharpening my teeth on all the curse words I wanted to say, I grumbled and turned away from the doors before I made a scene.

The building's security staff had originally worked for my mother. She claimed they were a gift to celebrate construction finally coming to an end, but I knew the truth. They were not only meant to keep me safe, but also report my every move.

Sometimes it seemed like my mother knew the details of my life better than I did.

Traveling up a private elevator that required a key, I finally stepped into the closest thing I had to a home.

I'd saved the best part of the building for myself, turning the space inside the dome into my personal sanctuary. Terracotta brick lined the walls, and black iron support beams had been left exposed. Two stories fit inside the dome. Extra walls had been erected on the first floor to create traditionally sized rooms that housed the kitchen, sitting room, office, and extra bedroom.

No member of my family had ever been allowed to set foot in this apartment, and I swept the place regularly for hidden devices. I wasn't naive enough to think this would stop my family from knowing what went on inside my home, but it at least gave me the illusion of privacy.

I made a direct line for the kitchen, pulled a random bottle out of the wine fridge, and poured myself a drink. Throwing my head back, I downed half the glass in one go, drowning myself in the fragrance of black cherries.

Mellow acid lingered on my tongue as I looked down into the glass. My own distorted reflection stared back at me.

"Fuck."

I flung the glass across the room, where it smashed against the wall. "That smug, disgusting... Fuck."

Red wine dripped down the terracotta walls, catching and pooling in the brick's rough texture. Garrison watched the wine's slow descent until it reached the floor.

"Do you have a broom?"

I pointed toward the correct closet, and Garrison retrieved an armload of cleaning supplies.

The man first removed his suit jacket, which he folded and left on a chair, then started to calmly sweep up the broken glass.

"This is because of your uncle, I assume."

Running a shaking hand through my hair, I recorked the wine and stored it away before I did something regrettable. Like throwing the entire bottle.

"Yeah. I hate him. Every time I see his face, I want to wring his damn neck."

I would never have let my family see such a display of emotion. But this was my home. It was safe to express myself here. I'd developed a habit of retreating behind these familiar walls whenever negative emotions built up under my skin and I needed to let them run free without fear of judgment.

It wasn't until the wine glass had already left my hand that I remembered Garrison could see me as well, but it was too late to stuff the anger back inside its cage.

Once the glass was dealt with, Garrison turned a wet rag on the wall to wipe away the wine.

"Is this how you usually deal with anger, or is your uncle a special case? I just want to know how often I'll need to duck flying glassware."

With a hollow sound of bone against wood, I leaned back and let my head knock against the kitchen cupboard.

"No. When I'm agitated I usually go to a club to blow off steam. But, I can't do that right now."

Still scrubbing at the wine stain, Garrison nodded as he and I spoke at the same time.

"It's not safe."

"It's two pm."

We both looked at each other, blinking through a moment of confusion.

The wine-stained rag made a wet splash when Garrison dropped it into a bucket of water. The fabric of his new shirt strained when he crossed his arms, almost distracting me from what the man said next.

"A club? You plan on going out tonight?"

I shrugged and wished I hadn't put the wine bottle away. It would have given me something to do with my hands as I faced Garrison's obvious disdain. "You saw my uncle. He's infuriating. I need to blow off some steam, and going out to a club is a good way to do that."

It didn't seem possible, but Garrison somehow seemed to draw himself together and appear a little bigger. "The last time you were at a club someone almost killed you."

Since the shirt wasn't tailored, it struggled to contain the width of Garrison's shoulders. The top button seemed ready to pop open at any moment.

My restless fingers found an outlet. Stepping into Garrison's personal space, I toyed with the buttons running down the man's shirt. They wouldn't need much coaxing to fall open, practically begging to reveal the impressive chest underneath.

"If you want to keep me on house arrest, then you're responsible for entertaining me. I'm a nightmare when I'm bored."

Garrison grabbed my hand before I could undo the button.

"It seems like you're always a nightmare."

The heel of Garrison's shoe knocked against the bucket when I pushed him back, sloshing red-tinted water over the floor.

"Because I'm usually bored. That's why I like you. You're not boring."

Although Garrison was much broader than me, we had only a few inches of difference in height. So, when I hooked a hand around the back of Garrison's neck, I didn't have to pull the other man down very far for our lips to meet.

Just as I suspected, Garrison's muscular frame was a delight to press up against. Like the unyielding trunk of a tree that I couldn't wait to climb.

Yet, the other man didn't respond. Garrison's lips remained unmoving, and he barely seemed to breathe.

I pulled away and looked up into a set of confused eyes. "What? You're not... Did I misread something here?"

Only a few inches away, Garrison's

hands hovered in the air like he wasn't sure what to do with them. "You were being serious. I thought you were just having fun flirting."

"I was having fun flirting, and I'd like to have fun doing other things. What's the problem? Do you not want to?"

"I'm not..." Garrison trailed off and knelt to fix the bucket he'd knocked over. When he finally spoke, his voice was directed at the floor. "I'm a lot older than you."

It was actually kind of cute, seeing such a strong man suddenly look nervous. In all of my fantasies, I'd imagined Garrison as a dominant force in bed, but I could work with this newfound shyness as well.

I knelt down so I was eye level with Garrison and took the bucket from his hands, placing it out of the way. "A few years between us doesn't matter. I know your age, and I've decided that I want you. That's my decision. You don't get to make it for me. The only decisions you get to make are your own." Grabbing Garrison's wrists, I coaxed the other man to his feet. "So, now that you know where I stand, what do you want?"

Lines appeared on either side of Garrison's mouth as his expression pinched. "I'm not sure how much I can promise you."

"Not looking for promises. Just a good fuck."

When Garrison was deep in thought, he stopped blinking, like he was afraid to miss a single detail as he weighed his options. This gave me an unimpeded view of the man's eyes. They looked vacant, like a house without lights, as Garrison's thoughts turned inward. His eyes weren't truly black, but rather a very dark brown. From such a short distance, I could see flecks of gold scattered around the edges. I wondered how many people had seen Garrison from this intimate perspective. The man didn't seem like the type to let others close very easily.

Had previous lovers stared into the man's eyes and admired the secret treasure that I had found, or had they seen only a dark void?

After a few moments, light returned to Garrison's eyes, making the flecks of gold sparkle.

"Sleeping with my new employer is probably a bad idea." The smallest of smiles graced his lips. "But I've spent my whole life following *good* ideas, and still got burned in the end. So, maybe a bad idea is what I need."

At the mention of burns, my thoughts turned toward the scars covering Garrison's back. I really wanted to ask about the wounds that caused those marks but refrained. I hadn't known Garrison long, but I could already tell that such an invasive question would only push the man away from me.

Instead, I fisted both hands in the front of Garrison's shirt, popping a few of the already strained buttons. "Lucky for you, I'm a master of bad ideas."

I crashed our mouths together again. This time the heat was matched from both sides. Garrison's hands settled on my waist like a vice grip of hot iron. Wrapping my arms around the other man's neck, I pulled us closer together until not a molecule of air could have fit between our bodies.

Our kiss deepened, lips parting and tongues sliding against each other. I moaned when my growing arousal rubbed against Garrison's hip. Fire blossomed in my veins. My head spun even with my eyes closed.

We both pulled away at the same time, panting for air. Before Garrison could fully escape, I nipped the man's bottom lip.

"Come on. This'll be more comfortable upstairs."

I didn't wait for an answer. I didn't need one. The look in Garrison's eyes was too eager to mean anything but "yes".

With me leading the way, the two of us headed to the apartment's second floor. The master bedroom took up the entire space. Practically its own little studio apartment, the curved dome of the ceiling gave it a unique look. There were no windows on the walls. Instead, rays of afternoon sunlight streamed in through a round skylight cut into the middle of the dome. It was framed by black iron that extended down and joined together into a complex support pole at the center of the room. More black bars extended from the edge of the window frame, creating a curved pattern over the terracotta walls that resembled a metal spider web.

Garrison turned in slow circles to take in the full view.

"Interesting design choice."

"More of a necessity than a choice." I flicked a switch on the wall and an automated shade covered the skylight. "The pole at the center couldn't be removed, but adding a skylight was the only way to get some natural light in here without compromising the structure. So, the architect designed a support system that branched around the window and extended down the curve of the dome."

A dimmer switch on the room's remaining lights created an artificial dusk. We could still see, but the dim atmosphere softened harsh edges and gave everything a dreamlike quality.

"It was a construction nightmare, but fortuitous in the end. I wasn't certain about it at first. Now I quite like it."

"It suits you."

Under different circumstances, I would have admired how easily the other man fit inside my personal space. At the moment, however, the fire smoldering in my gut drew my attention elsewhere. I couldn't stop staring at the way Garrison's shirt strained across his chest with each movement. From now on, all of Garrison's clothing would need to be tailored, or I was going to be trapped in a state of perpetual arousal.

I licked my dry lips before speaking.

"I'm glad you think so. Now, are we going to keep discussing interior design, or are you going to come over here?"

Finally, Garrison stopped looking around the room and turned his attention back where it belonged. Firmly fixed on me. Our eyes met and a spark passed between us.

As much as I wanted to just grab the man, I waited for Garrison to come to me.

It was a short wait.

Garrison's long legs took only a few strides to bring him into my arms. Our lips found each other easily, hotter and heavier than before. Tongues danced and breath mingled. The spark between us ignited, and I felt burned from the inside out.

Large hands tangled in my shoulder length hair, locking my head in place as I was devoured. I was already panting from just a kiss.

How much better would it be once our clothes were off?

Time to find out.

With the ripping of fabric and buttons, Garrison's shirt floated to the floor in pieces. I smirked against our kiss when Garrison barely seemed to notice. I would need to give Raymond an extra-large tip. The tailor was going to be very busy.

The kiss ended, but I stayed close enough for our lips to brush. "Still not enough."

Then, without warning, I shoved Garrison back toward the bed. It took all of my strength to knock the other man off balance, and even that couldn't get the job done. There was an obvious moment where Garrison could have caught himself.

Instead, he shifted his feet and let himself fall.

The bed bounced when Garrison landed flat on his back, arms splayed haphazardly to his sides. I immediately followed, straddling his hips and kissing him hard enough to press him into the mattress.

"That's better," I said when I abandoned Garrison's mouth to spread kisses down the man's neck. "More access."

I nearly ripped my own shirt as I slid the offending garment off my shoulders while trailing more kisses over Garrison's chest. Reaching the center of one well-defined pec, I bit the flesh beneath my mouth.

"You know, you could help."

This finally stirred Garrison from his stunned state. The man's hands became flurry of motion, attacking the fastenings for both of our pants.

Working together, we managed to discard all of our clothes. Everything ended up on the floor, except for Garrison's knee brace. That stayed firmly in place.

I pressed a quick kiss to one of the ugly scars running under a strap, then moved on to more important things.

Like the slide of flesh against flesh as I straddled Garrison's hips once again.

This time my body was on full display. I shivered as I felt the path of Garrison's eyes over my skin, starting at my chest and slowly moving downward.

It took longer than expected for Garrison to notice the special surprise waiting under my clothing. Normally, it was one of the first things to grab people's attention, but Garrison seemed so distracted by the lines of my legs that he complexly skipped over what lay between them. When the man finally did notice, his sudden gasp sent me rocking forward.

The silver hoop in my eyebrow wasn't my only piercing.

Dragging one hand along my own thigh—since Garrison seemed to like my legs so much— I stroked one finger up the length of my cock. My movements were deliberate, showing off the three barbell piercings along the underside of my shaft.

"See something interesting?"

Swallowing hard, Garrison nodded. He reached up to wrap one hand around my cock, broad palm covering most of the shaft. With his thumb, he toyed with one of the piercings, pressing the ball bearing on the end back and forth.

I gasped when the surprisingly delicate touch sent fire licking up my spine.

"Wait. Stop."

Garrison's hand immediately froze. I wanted to weep at the sudden loss of stimulation, but forced myself to pull Garrison's hand away from my cock.

"Sorry, but if you keep doing that, this isn't going to last long. How about this?"

Grabbing each of the man's wrists, I guided Garrison's hands to the wrought iron headboard.

"Hold on, and don't let go."

Nodding, Garrison laced his fingers through the metal bars and gripped tight to the frame.

Ideally, I would have liked to tie Garrison to the bed. I had some restraints stored in a nearby drawer, but I didn't think we were ready for that. Such submission would require a level of trust neither of us were ready for yet. Maybe in the future. For now, I would make do with the honor system.

From there, it became a game. I slowly slid down Garrison's body, running my mouth over his neck and chest and stomach in a search for sensitive spots. Tugging with my teeth on one of Garrison's nipples earned me a slight gasp. Running my tongue over the edges of well-defined abs caused Garrison to laugh, which wasn't what I wanted. My goal was to find Garrison's limit and make the man lose control.

I hit paydirt when my hand brushed over a long, jagged scar low on Garrison's hip. The man's whole body jerked, and he nearly let go of the headboard.

I could feel a grin pulling at my face, no doubt making me look like a lecherous

Cheshire cat. Letting our bodies rub together, I moved down farther until my face was only inches from Garrison's hip.

With my lips and tongue, I teased the uneven texture of the scar. Above me, out of my line of sight, Garrison let out a moan. The longer I kept up my attack, the more out of breath Garrison sounded until the larger man was practically writhing against the sheets. I pressed down on Garrison's hips, pinning the man to the bed. Then, still with my mouth, I followed the line of the scar like an arrow pointing me to my final goal.

Garrison's cock stood hard and eager against his stomach, already leaking pre-cum over his abs.

This part of Garrison's anatomy was as tall and thick as everything else on the man, and I was delighted to find him uncircumcised. With the broad flat of my tongue, I licked a stripe up the shaft of Garrison's cock. Then I laughed when Garrison started cursing.

"It's been a while for you, hasn't it? You're more sensitive than I expected."

Garrison gasped for air, filling his lungs to capacity as he struggled to calm down. "Honestly... can't remember the last time I was with someone."

I hummed low in my throat, letting my lips brush the head of Garrison's cock so the other man could feel the vibrations. "Better prepare yourself then. This is gonna be fun."

Taking a deep breath, I swallowed as much of Garrison as I could in one go. I only managed about half before it hit the back of my throat and I had to stop. Still, it was enough to have Garrison writhing like an electric eel.

With slow, careful movements, I started bobbing my head up and down, letting Garrison's cock slide between my lips and laving over the head with my tongue.

Garrison moaned and cursed again. His voice cut off like he was being strangled when I sped up.

Usually, due to my family heritage, people were eager to fall on their knees for me. I never got to be on the giving side of the exchange, and I'd forgotten how much I enjoyed it. Having this level of control over my partner's pleasure could easily become an addiction.

A pair of hands gripped my hair. Abandoning Garrison's cock, I scowled up at the other man.

"Put your hands back where they belong."

It took several moments, and a few deep breaths, for Garrison to process what I said. When he did, his hands shot back up to the headboard so quickly his knuckles banged against the metal.

I smirked. "Good boy."

Then I returned to sucking Garrison's cock with a vengeance.

This time, I managed to swallow most of it, sending Garrison into a writhing fit. The man cursed, and even pleaded, which in turn made my own arousal twist tighter in my gut. I rutted against Garrison's leg, teasing myself while simultaneously speeding up the motion of my head.

An inorganic groan of metal caught my attention and I pulled away again.

Garrison was gripping the iron headboard so tightly he'd bent one of the smaller bars out of shape.

The man hadn't even noticed what he'd done. His eyes were closed, and he seemed to be talking himself through a series of breathing exercises. Sweat dripped over flushed skin, catching in the dip between his pecs as his chest heaved.

My throat suddenly went dry. I swallowed several times and licked my lips as I fought to control the arousal pooling in my brain. Garrison was stronger than any man who had submitted to me before. I needed to feel that strength beneath me.

Fishing out a few supplies from the bedside table, I returned to straddling Garrison's thighs. "Just give me a minute, big guy. Then we can really get started."

With practiced movements, I rolled a condom down over Garrison's cock. Maybe someday we could forgo such protection, but just like the restraints I wanted to use, we weren't at that level of trust yet.

By then, Garrison had calmed down enough to watch with eager eyes as I poured lubricant over my own fingers. Knowing I had an audience, I made a production out of reaching behind myself and rubbing the lube around the rim of my hole. Little sparks of pleasure raced up my spine, but they only served to whet my appetite.

Garrison was a feast, and I wouldn't be satisfied until I glutted myself on the man.

With a moan, I slipped two fingers inside myself and scissored them open to stretch my internal muscles. This was even worse. It felt like a watered-down version of the stretch I really wanted. Impatience built like a ball of pressure at the base of my skull.

Damn the limits of the human body.

I didn't take as much time preparing as I probably should have, given Garrison's size, but I couldn't wait. The moment I deemed myself stretched enough to avoid injury, I pulled out my fingers and shifted my hips. Garrison's cock pressed right up against my ass, seemingly just as eager as I felt.

In this position, with me sitting astride Garrison's hips, the other man had no choice but to wait for me to make the next move. Arousal turned into a rush of power greater than any I'd known in my mafia-fueled life.

Oh, yes, this could definitely become an addiction.

Without a word of warning, I let my hips drop and impaled myself on Garrison's cock. It was painful, as expected, but also so good. I moaned and shuddered, clenching my internal muscles around the intrusion, which dragged a groan out of Garrison as well.

As the pain faded, I raised myself up until the head of Garrison's cock barely remained inside me. I paused just long enough to see the other man squirm, then I plunged down again.

Garrison shouted and I threw my head back as pleasure sang through my veins. The thick girth of Garrison's arousal spread me open without mercy, like being fucked by an iron bar. Biting my lip, I breathed deep through my nose, then repeated the action.

Slow up, and quick down.

Over and over.

Each time Garrison seemed to hit a little deeper, until I expected to feel the outline of the man's cock through my skin when I pressed a hand to my own stomach.

"Fuck." I nearly bit my tongue on the curse word as I started bouncing wildly. "Fuck. You're so... so much. Too much. I need more."

Our momentum shifted when Garrison bucked his hips up at the same time I dropped down. The added force sent his cock slamming right into my prostate.

Ecstasy flooded my brain, nearly making me come on the spot. I braced my hands on Garrison's chest to keep myself upright.

"Ah. Right there. Yes."

My legs trembled and my muscles locked up; I was unable to move.

Yet, Garrison didn't stop. The man kept thrusting upward, digging his heels into the mattress for more leverage even as he dutifully maintained his grip on the headboard.

Sitting atop Garrison as the man fucked up into me was like riding a bucking bronco without a saddle. I clung to Garrison's shoulders to maintain my seat on the wild ride. Through sheer will, I managed to start moving my hips again. I met Garrison thrust for thrust as we pushed each other toward the height of pleasure just out of reach.

Garrison didn't say a word. He made plenty of noise, grunts and groans and moans, but he didn't talk much during sex.

That was fine. I babbled enough for the both of us.

"Come on, baby." My nails clawed red streaks over Garrison's chest. "I can tell you're close. Give it to me."

White lights danced around the edges of my vision. I didn't dare look away from the pleasure illuminating Garrison's face. It took all of my control to push back the orgasm building under my skin and in my belly. I wanted to see Garrison finish first.

Metal bent even more under Garrison's straining grip as the man approached his end.

When the moment finally came, it was beautiful. As Garrison was lost in his own small death, the lines of his face softened. Even the scar cutting down his cheek seemed to diminish.

Fucking myself down on Garrison as the other man rode out the last waves of orgasm, I tumbled over the edge of my own peak. My thighs clenched tight around Garrison's hips, locking us together. Every nerve in my body erupted at the same time. It seemed to go on forever, crashing over me in waves. Each time I thought it was over, I'd be pulled back into the tide of pleasure.

Eventually, it ended and my heart rate returned to normal, though it took several minutes for my thoughts to return from the gray haze they'd wandered off into.

When I could properly think again, I looked down at the man below me and immediately started laughing.

"I'm so sorry."

My apology lost its effect when I could barely form the words through my laughter.

Grumbling under his breath, Garrison released the headboard to wipe the results of my orgasm off his face.

"At least I'll know it's coming next time."

My laughter died, replaced by a bloom of warmth taking root behind my breastbone. We hadn't discussed "next time". For Garrison to make such an assumption had to mean the man could also see himself as a staple in my life.

Together we managed to disentangle ourselves and clean up. By then it was barely mid-afternoon, but I was already exhausted. A nap sounded perfect. I invited Garrison to join me, which the man accepted with little persuasion. We lay together in the dim light of the bedroom, still undressed, close enough for our legs to intertwine despite the bed being more than big enough for two people.

Garrison stretched out on his stomach with his folded arms acting as a pillow. His eyes were closed, but he was obviously still awake based on his breathing pattern. The bed sheet barely covered his hips, leaving his back on full display.

It was an invitation I couldn't refuse. I lay on my side with my head propped up on one hand while my other traced the burn scars on Garrison's back.

Without opening his eyes, Garrison pressed his shoulder blade more firmly into my palm. "If you're going to ask, just ask. I don't mind."

A tempting offer. One that I almost accepted. I followed the scars with my fingers until the rippled skin disappeared under the sheet, then I switched to drawing circles on Garrison's upper arm instead.

"What's the meaning of this tattoo?"

I noticed the design before but hadn't given it much thought. A tattoo was a choice, so it hadn't seemed as important as the remnants of unwanted injuries. However, now that I got a closer look, my interest was piqued.

Pairs of identical boots were arranged

in a ring around Garrison's right biceps. Each boot pair had a rifle sticking up from the center, and a helmet balanced on top of the gun.

This time, Garrison did open his eyes, though his gaze stayed rooted on the wall.

"It's a battlefield cross. They mark soldiers that have been killed."

It was then that I noticed a name on the side of one of the guns written in barely visible font. Checking the other guns, I found different names in the same places.

I wanted to know, but I couldn't ask. Even if Garrison was willing to tell me, that was a level of intimacy we weren't ready for.

Placing a quick kiss to the tattoo, I let the matter drop.

We lay in silence, listening to nothing but the sounds of our own breathing.

I was half asleep when an unexpected question from Garrison broke the quiet atmosphere.

"So, who is Valente to you? Because he seems to hate me, and if he's going to be around a lot that could be a problem."

Snapped out of my thoughts, I patted Garrison's shoulder. "It's not you. Valente was my father's... is my father's right-hand man. He's loyal to my family and dislikes all outsiders. Pretty sure he'd hate me too if I didn't have Russo blood in my veins."

That seemed to shock Garrison. Not outwardly, the man's face was a stoic and unreadable mask, but his body told a different story. Under my hand, the muscles of Garrison's back tensed.

"Hate you? Why? If anything he seems protective of you."

"Valente is protective of my family. Not me. He hates me because I'm gay. He's never said it out loud, but he gets this look on his face every time my sexuality comes up."

Garrison's head rose up from his arms and he glanced at the space between our bodies. Or the lack of space, as it was.

"If he's homophobic and protective of your family, then he's really going to hate me. The gay stranger who seduced you into bed."

The ridiculousness of such a statement gave me no choice. I had to retaliate with a kiss. It was a chaste exchange compared to our previous kisses. Our lips parted just enough for a quick slip of tongues before it ended.

"Pretty sure I'm the one who did the seducing."

"I don't think your man is going to see it like that."

A shiver shot up my spine at the implication of Garrison's words. "Don't call Valente *my man*. It sounds weird. You're my man. I hired you. You belong to me. Valente works for my father. That's all."

Garrison rarely let himself show big expressions. So, the smirk that lifted his lips, although small, was a maniacal grin by comparison.

"So, he's your father's man."

The image that came to mind caused another shiver to spread over my skin, leaving goosebumps in its wake. "Stop it. You're making it worse."

Garrison opened his mouth to speak again, but I cut him off by kissing him. It was an idle exchange, not meant to incite anything more. One kiss led to two, and then three. Then the kisses bled together and weren't worth counting.

Under the sheets, I rubbed my leg over Garrison's calf, seeking comfort in the slide of skin against skin. My thigh brushed the edge of Garrison's knee brace.

Like the tattoo, I'd also seen the brace before and dismissed it. Now it sparked my imagination.

Was it also the result of a combat injury?

Would Garrison ever tell me the stories behind all his scars?

The kiss continued, and I slid my hand down until it found one of the many scars decorating Garrison's body. This one was shaped like a starburst and lay in the hollow of Garrison's shoulder.

I loved these scars.

Each one brought a little spark of hope that Garrison could understand the violent life I came from. Maybe, once I scraped up the courage to admit who I really was, I wouldn't have to lose the man I'd just found.

CHAPTER EIGHT

Garrison

I HAD PLANNED to return to my apartment at some point, but after falling into bed with Alex, we'd ended up spending the rest of the day and night together.

It hadn't all been sex, though there had been several rounds of that. Later in the evening, Alex had to make a series of phone calls, and several packages arrived for me. Raymond must have worked overtime to get all of my clothing tailored in a matter of hours. However, no quality had been sacrificed for speed. When I tried on the suits and other outfits, they all fit perfectly.

Before I knew it, morning had come, and Alex and I had spent nearly twenty-four hours together.

As we were eating breakfast, the apartment's intercom rang. Alex answered it, then a few moments later met someone at the door. He never let them inside, just spoke with them across the threshold before accepting a box and closing the door again.

Back at the kitchen table, he handed the box to me. "Here. I've got a meeting today, and you're going to need these."

At first, I thought the tailor had forgotten something, but when I opened the box, I didn't find clothes inside.

The box was filled with weapons.

Nothing spectacular. Just a standard Glock with several styles of holsters, and a few combat knives that could be hidden in different places around my body.

No, the weapons themselves weren't a problem. As a bodyguard, it was expected for me to be armed.

The speed at which these weapons had been procured, however, was a concern. Especially with guns, proper licensing took time. I wasn't in the military anymore, and a lot more paperwork was needed for civilians to carry weapons.

When I asked about this, Alex claimed that I would have to speak with Valente. The man was in charge of security for everyone in the Mariano family, and that included weaponry.

In the end, I gave up asking, but vowed to demand answers from Valente the next time I saw the man.

When Alex and I were alone, it was easy to forget the situation that brought us together. However, the world kept spinning even when we weren't paying attention. Someone had tried to kill Alex. My first instinct was to keep Alex safe and locked away, but that wasn't possible. Alex had a family business to run.

So, I dressed in one of the new tailored suits, strapped on the provided weapons, and prepared to stand as Alex's bodyguard.

I'd expected a business meeting to take place in an office. Instead, Alex's driver took us just across the border into New York and dropped us off at an aquarium.

"Offices are boring," Alex said with a shrug. "Besides, the people I'm meeting today aren't exactly friendly. They do business with my family, but they're more like rivals than allies. Meeting on neutral ground like this keeps everything... civil."

Family?

The choice of words caught my attention.

Every time Alex mentioned his family business, he always put more emphasis on the family than the business. Most of the time he seemed to forget that there even was a business, referring to family matters and business matters like they were the same thing.

My hand drifted toward the new gun strapped to my hip.

The front of the aquarium was locked, but Alex led us around to a side door. To no one's surprise, we found Valente already waiting for us.

"Everything is prepared. The others arrived just a few minutes ago."

He gave me a short, pointed look before holding open the door.

I bit my tongue to silence the questions I wanted to ask and followed Alex inside.

Like most aquariums, the lights were turned down low to highlight the various tanks. We stepped into a world of contrasting shadows and lights. There was no one else around, but I still kept my voice to a whisper as I spoke to Alex. "What's prepared? Something I should know about?"

Bright blue light from a nearby tank illuminated one side of Alex's face. The rippling water created a pattern like scales on his skin.

"Valente has set up our own security around the building. The aquarium doesn't open for another hour, so we don't need to worry about crowds, but we still want to be safe." He stopped to coo over some small orange fish in a nearby tank, rubbing one finger on the glass like he was scratching behind a dog's ear.

I had never cared about fish, but it was endearing to watch the small creatures gather near Alex's finger to investigate the movement.

"Do you like fish?"

"Sort of." Alex left the small tank behind and headed farther into the building. "Mostly, I like the atmosphere in these kinds of places. It's soothing. Like being under water without needing to swim."

"If you like it so much, we'll have to

come back when someone isn't trying to kill you."

The words were out of my mouth before I could think them through. I schooled my face into a blank mask to keep from blushing.

How could I be so presumptuous?

At the end of the day, the two of us were employer and bodyguard. Nothing more. Sure, we slept together, but satisfying physical needs did not equate to an emotional connection.

Luckily, Alex didn't take offense. If anything, the man's smile grew wider.

He bumped his hip against me. "Careful. That almost sounded like you were asking me on a date." Despite the warning words, Alex's tone and the soft look in his eyes were clear invitations.

Taking a risk, I hooked one finger in Alex's belt loop and pulled the other man closer. "Keep yourself alive and we'll see what happens."

If we were alone, we would have kissed. However, Valente remained only a few steps behind, so we parted just enough to maintain public decency.

That didn't stop Alex from grumbling under his breath. "Ugh. Fuck this meeting."

From what I had understood based on overheard phone calls, Alex had been the one to set up the meeting. Curious, I couldn't help but ask, "Is this meeting really necessary?"

We passed by a large cylindrical tank full of floating jellyfish. Each of us stepped to a different side of the cylinder so we were divided by clear walls of glass and water.

Moving currents distorted Alex's face like a mirage, but the heavy sigh he expressed was unmistakable.

"Unfortunately, yes. My family has worked with these two for a long time. I need to establish myself with them if I'm going to be in charge of things while my father is indisposed."

Between us, dozens of jellyfish glowed in the colored light shining from above. Their boneless forms drifted in circles, slaves to the gentle current of their environment.

Luckily, although the tank was tall, it wasn't very wide. The two of us passed by the barrier quickly and came together once again.

I let my pinky brush the side of Alex's

hand in an almost invisible show of support. "If you can't avoid it, then let's get it over with. Go in there, make your presence known, and then we can do something more entertaining afterward."

Even in the dim light of the aquarium, Alex's eyes smoldered like twin coals as they traveled up and down my body.

"I think I made a mistake hiring you. How am I supposed to concentrate when you're putting thoughts in my head?"

I didn't bother responding. We both knew Alex was being rhetorical, but it was thrilling to think that just a few words from me could distract the other man to such a degree.

At the far back of the aquarium, we found the largest tank in the building. The size of a three-story house, it had a completely black backdrop with only jagged rocks and sand for decoration. Dozens of sharks swam through the open water, slipping in and out of the shadows.

Rows upon rows of benches sat before the main wall of the tank, stacked like an auditorium. Signage on the wall advertised the area as a stage for underwater shows.

Two people waited right in front of the

tank.

A man stood near the clear wall, watching the underwater predators with genuine interest. He was tall and thin, with an olive complexion similar to Alex. However, his blue eyes spoke of a mixed heritage.

A woman sat on the lowest row of benches. Her harsh bob haircut and sharp cheekbones made her look like the human embodiment of a knife. Even her nails, which she tapped impatiently on the bench, were blood red and filed to sharp points.

When Alex stepped into the room, both the man and woman turned toward him with such synchronized movements it seemed rehearsed.

I hung back at the edge of the benches as Alex approached the pair. From this distance, I couldn't hear what they said but I was glad to see confidence flowing through Alex with every step.

It was one less thing to worry about.

The layout of the room unnerved me. There were too many doors and high vantage points. No matter which way Alex turned, his back was always vulnerable.

At least a dozen people stood stationed

around the room like silent watchmen.

Were all of these Valente's men, or did some of them work for the people Alex was meeting?

I had no way of knowing.

A rough hand grabbed my arm and dragged me away from the benches. I unlocked the holster on my gun before I realized it was Valente who had grabbed me. That fact didn't completely ease my fears, but I kept my gun holstered as we stepped into the far corner.

Valente spit his words through clenched teeth. "Stop being so indecent."

I flexed my arm, but I didn't try to pull it out of Valente's grip.

Although past his prime, the man still had incredible strength. He must have been an absolute powerhouse when he was younger. Even now, he was not someone I wanted to fight one-on-one.

"What are you talking about?"

Valente's grip tightened. "You're a whore with a gun who doesn't know his place, and Alex is too inexperienced to correct you. So, I will. Whatever dalliance the two of you have going needs to stop."

Ah, so Alex was right. Valente was just a bigot who hated that Alex was gay.

Having me around only increased that hate as it put Alex's sexuality on display.

I sighed and tried not to roll my eyes. There was nothing I could do to solve that problem. The man hated me for simply existing, and no action on my part could change that.

Ignoring the hand still holding my arm, I turned to keep one eye on Valente and one eye on Alex. The tank wall had been built with a curve, which cut off my view to part of the room from this corner.

"We've done nothing wrong, and we're not harming anyone."

Alex moved closer to the dark-haired man by the tank wall, putting him right at the edge of my sight.

A particularly large shark swam close to the glass, showing off its rows of teeth like it knew it had an audience. In a different situation the smile that graced Alex's face at the sight of the predatory fish would have been endearing. Right now, I just wanted him to pay better attention to his surroundings. There were too many people in this room that I didn't know.

Even Valente, one of the few people I did know, didn't seem to be on Alex's side at the moment. The man was more interested in berating me than guarding Alex, as if being gay posed a greater threat than a bullet to the head.

"You are harming this family. Carrying on such a disgusting affair in public will destroy Alex's reputation with the other families. They'll lose respect for him, and so, lose respect for the Mariano name. They may even refuse to do business with him."

I nodded along, barely paying attention to what Valente was saying. I was too busy cataloging everyone in the room, trying to judge based on body posture who was an ally or an enemy.

"Who's that?" I asked, indicating one of the nameless security personnel standing on the other side of the room.

Valente practically hissed in anger. "Are you even listening?"

I barely glanced at the man, too focused on the rest of the room. "No, I'm not. Answer the question. Who's that? Are they one of our people?"

Grumbling insults under his breath, Valente looked at the person in question. "Yes, that's a member of our security. Why?"

Dread stretched its icy fingers through my gut. "They're positioned wrong."

I charged forward, intending to get Alex out of danger, but Valente yanked me back. "What are you doing? Don't interrupt."

Turning on Valente with one hand already on my gun, I barely stopped myself from punching the other man in the face.

"That man of yours is positioned wrong. They're too far from the door, and they can't see most of the room from where they're standing. From that angle they only have a clear view of one thing. The back of Alex's head."

Too late.

Even as I spoke, I saw the suspicious man pull out a palm-sized gun. It was the kind of weapon perfect for assassinations as it was easily overlooked, but a small bullet could still kill someone.

There was no time to reach Alex now. Instead, I drew my own gun.

"Alex, get down!"

Thankfully, Alex listened without question and dropped to the floor just before the assassin pulled the trigger.

In the same breath, I fired my own

gun, striking the assassin in the shoulder. The man fell, possibly dead, but I was too busy running to Alex's side to care.

"Are you all right?"

"Yeah, I'm fine." Alex pointed to the bullet lodged in the side of the tank. "They missed." Such thick acrylic was stronger than it looked, even against a gunshot. The tank was in no danger of breaking but every shark in the vicinity had scattered to the farthest shadows.

Another gunshot had us both instinctually ducking. Someone cried out in pain. I pulled Alex down behind a bench and peered over the edge.

The dark-haired man clutched his arm. He'd been grazed by a bullet. Without knowing where the shot came from, it was impossible to tell if he had been the original target or was just an unlucky casualty.

Several people swarmed the man, shielding him as they pulled him from the room.

I gripped Alex's arm, intending to do the same. "Come on. We need to get you out of here."

More bullets flew above our heads. We

stayed behind the cover of the bench, inching our way toward the nearest door.

The sound of a gun firing from the opposite direction brought us to a halt.

Valente stood at the center of the room, shooting at several targets at once. "Go on." He pulled the trigger again and someone shouted in pain just out of sight. "I'll cover you."

We sprinted for the door, with me shielding Alex as much as I could.

Various tanks and exhibits passed by in a blur as we ran from room to room. The aquarium, which had been so friendly before, was now a twisted labyrinth of shadows and strange geometry that hindered our escape at every turn.

In the middle of an underwater tunnel, our sprint came to a stop. Coral stood to either side, and a group of three armed individuals blocked the path in front. Turning around, we found another armed group waiting for us at the opposite end of the tunnel. We were trapped, pinned in by acrylic walls and deadly weapons.

No choice but to stand and fight.

Alex and I positioned ourselves back-to-back, each facing down one side of the tunnel.

I gripped my gun, finger poised on the trigger. If I was fast, I could probably take out two or three of them before they got too close. It might give Alex enough opportunity to escape, especially if I stayed behind to keep the remaining enemies busy.

Before I could voice this plan, however, Alex nudged me with an elbow. "Take care of your side. These ones are mine."

He charged down the tunnel before I could stop him. Alex had no gun, only a thin silver knife clutched in one hand. It should have been easy for someone to shoot him, but the man was impossibly fast. I knew Alex was fit, I'd explored the other man's body in close detail, but this exceeded my expectations.

In a blur of motion, Alex stabbed his knife through the wrist of the first enemy as they raised their gun. Blood sprayed from the wound, meaning he'd managed to hit an artery on the first stab. It was an incredible show of precision, executed in the blink of an eye.

I couldn't watch any longer. I had my own threat to deal with.

The enemies at the other end of the tunnel were farther away. I fired in their general direction while dodging to the side. My shot didn't hit anything, but it delayed them long enough for me to close the distance.

Forgoing weapons entirely, I slammed a fist into the face of the first person I reached. The man's jaw snapped and he screamed. Blood dribbled down his chin, and several teeth landed on the floor.

I kicked the fucker out of the way and kept going.

Guns were mostly useless in close combat, so I pulled out a knife strapped to the inside of my wrist. It was a short blade but had a serrated edge for maximum damage.

The second enemy managed to block my strike when I swung at his face. Feigning a step left, I spun on the ball of my foot and lunged to the right instead. The trick caught my opponent off guard just long enough for me to slip my knife between the man's ribs. The assailant didn't make a sound as his lungs suddenly deflated, but his face twisted in silent pain. One last breath rattled in his chest as he collapsed to the floor.

Two down, one to go.

The third opponent took advantage of

the distraction his fallen comrade had created to stab right for my heart. Blue aquarium light glinted off the edge of the blade, alerting me of the danger just in time. I jumped back, barely missing the fatal blow, but the knife still found my flesh just above the elbow.

Only years of combat experience kept me focused through the pain radiating up my arm. I grabbed the hand holding the knife before it could retreat and used it to drag my opponent closer. Hooking my other arm around the attacker, I threw the man over my shoulder and slammed him as hard as I could into the floor.

Something broke.

I heard the snap of bone when my opponent landed. Yet, it wasn't enough. The man was already trying to stumble to his feet.

Before he could stand and restart the fight, I slammed my boot into the man's temple. The blow knocked the assailant out cold.

With the threat eliminated, I looked toward Alex and froze in shock.

Two of Alex's opponents lay on the floor, sliced to ribbons. I would have thought they were mauled by a jungle cat, based on the numerous cuts on their face and arms. An impressive amount of blood pooled beneath their bodies, implying at least one serious injury on each of them.

The third opponent was pinned to the wall with Alex's hand on the man's throat. As I watched, Alex raised his knife and stabbed it deep into his attacker's gut.

"Who sent you? How did you know I would be here?"

Alex didn't shout. He didn't need to. His face was only inches from his opponent's ear.

Bloody fingers clawed at Alex's hand. The pinned enemy could barely suck in enough air to spit out two words. "F... uck. Yo... u."

In response, Alex relaxed his grip on the man's throat, but pressed his knife deeper into his stomach. "Don't be like that. Gut wounds are fatal, but they take forever. There's still time to get you to a doctor. If you tell me what I want, I might be merciful."

The person thought for a moment, then smiled with a mouthful of bloody teeth. They cackled and spat a glob of red-tinted saliva in Alex's face.

A snarl of rage distorted Alex's

features. Pulling his knife out of the person's gut, he stabbed the blade directly into the man's face. Over and over the knife came down, until the person pinned to the wall barely looked human.

Once the enemy was definitely dead, Alex let the body drop to the floor. He stood in the middle of the tunnel, looking up at the water above as he sucked a deep breath in through his nose. With his unbloodied hand, he smoothed disheveled hair out of his face. Then, with a calm expression, he pulled out a handkerchief from the pocket of his jacket and started calmly cleaning his knife.

His hands never stopped moving as he glanced at my felled opponents. "Good job." Holding up his knife to the light, Alex deemed the blade clean enough and stored it and the cloth back inside his jacket. "Come on. Let's get out of here."

I hadn't moved an inch. I barely remembered to breathe. It was only muscle memory that allowed me to re-sheath my own knife without stabbing myself.

Logically, I'd always known Alex must have combat training. The man had been too accepting of the first assassination attempt. Such easy dismissal of violence only came from repeated exposure.

The bloody aftermath scattered over the floor, however, was something else. This was brutality on a level I had rarely seen.

Most shocking, however, was Alex's calm attitude afterward. Even hardened soldiers would balk after turning a man's face into bloody soup. Yet, Alex stepped over the bodies on the floor as if they weren't there and headed for the end of the tunnel.

He stopped only when he noticed I wasn't following. "What's wrong? Are you hurt?"

"Um..." I glanced down at the wound on my arm, barely feeling the pain. "Nothing serious."

Alex returned to my side, inspecting my injury with careful fingers. "Don't worry. We'll get you fixed up. My family's got several expert doctors on payroll."

Lacing our hands together, Alex led me through the tunnel and all the way out of the building.

I followed silently, numb from the brain down.

Outside, bright sunlight stung my eyes

after spending so long in the dark. I raised the hand not caught in Alex's grip to shade my eyes as I looked around. The street outside the aquarium looked undisturbed. There wasn't a hint of the brutal battle that had just taken place inside the building's walls.

As usual, a running car waited for us only a few feet away.

Alex slipped into the backseat, dragging me with him. He told the driver to take us back to his apartment, then collapsed back into his seat and groaned.

"That was a nightmare." He ran his hands through his hair, tugging at his scalp in frustration. "Coming after me is one thing. But getting the Vidales and Bianchi families involved... Fuck. They're probably going to blame me, since I'm the one who initiated the meeting. God damn it."

I listened to Alex rant and touched the gun strapped to my hip with numb fingers.

The weapon had been procured too quickly, and I was starting to suspect how.

A thousand questions assaulted my brain at once, but I kept them all behind my teeth. This was not the kind of situation where answers could be demanded, but I also couldn't stay silent.

"Alex?" I tried to keep my expression neutral as I waited until I had the other man's attention. "We were just attacked. Aren't you going to call the police?"

Black eyes regarded me solemnly. I could almost see the wheels turning in their depths. Asking that question while trapped in Alex's car was probably a bad idea. It could even get me killed, but I refused to play the fool one moment longer.

Finally, after too much silence, Alex spoke.

"I think you already know the answer to that question."

Closing my eyes, I swallowed the knot that formed in my throat.

"No, you're not. Your... family will take care of it."

If I was smart, I would have bailed from the car right that moment. We weren't driving that fast. The fall wouldn't kill me.

However, I wanted answers.

Why had Alex even hired me in the first place?

Was this just a twisted game to keep the other man entertained?

Before I could ask any of these questions, Alex's phone rang.

Never breaking eye contact with me, Alex answered the phone with an angry swipe of his hand.

"What?"

A few words were spoken on the other side of the phone, too soft for me to hear.

Alex suddenly sat up straight. "You can't be... No."

The person on the line kept speaking, but Alex let the hand holding the phone drop to his lap.

As overwhelmed as I felt, Alex's reaction was too worrisome for me to ignore.

"What is it? What happened?"

Dark eyes looked at me again, their glittering depths now dull as obsidian.

Alex opened his mouth, closed it, then went back to staring at his phone.

Another silent moment passed, interrupted only by the rumble of the car's engine as it traveled through the city. I considered taking the phone and demanding answers from the person on the line when Alex finally spoke.

"My father is dead."

CHAPTER NINE

Alex

I DIDN'T REMEMBER telling my driver to change course, but an hour later the car approached the Mantoloking bridge. Appropriate to its name, the bridge led to Mantoloking township, where the Mariano family's other New Jersey house resided.

My mother would be waiting there. We had so many things to talk about, now that my father was dead.

Like, how the fuck did the man die in the first place?

Casualty of a prison riot?

That was a bold lie.

No, the man had been assassinated,

just like someone was trying to do to me.

Before we crossed the bridge, I told the driver to pull over on the side of the road. I needed a moment to breathe. Pushing my way out the door, I cursed when I tripped over the curb. Everything felt out of balance, like something inside my head had shifted sideways.

Bracing his elbows on the bridge railing, I breathed deep through my nose, filling my lungs with sea air. The bridge overlooked a marina filled with yachts. People scurried over the docks as they secured their boats against rolling waters.

Clouds covered the sun. A storm was coming. It wasn't here yet, but it would arrive sooner than people wanted.

Rough weather waited for no man.

Garrison stepped up next to me, posture straight as an iron rod.

"What's your plan, now?"

I couldn't watch the churning water anymore. I kept my gaze on the railing, picking at a splinter of wood sticking up from the edge.

"Plan? I don't know. My family has a house in Mantoloking. My mother is there right now. I need to meet with her and discuss... everything."

As I spoke, Garrison nodded along, but his gaze never left the waves below our feet.

"Your family. Were you ever going to tell me the truth about your family, or were you expecting me to stay ignorant?"

"Garrison, it's not..." I started to say, but I didn't know where the rest of the sentence was going. It didn't matter. Garrison interrupted before I could finish anyway, grabbing my arm and turning me around so we faced each other.

"Don't deflect. Tell me the truth. I want to hear it from your mouth. Who are you?"

It was surprisingly easy to look Garrison in the eye. "I'm Alex Mariano. Son of David Russo, who is the head of the Mariano family."

I squeezed the railing, and the loose splinter I'd been toying with pierced my skin. The prick of pain brought a moment of clarity.

"Or... my father *was* the head of the family. I guess I'm in charge now."

It shouldn't have been such a startling revelation. Technically, I'd been acting as the head of the family since my father's recent arrest. That was the very reason I'd set up a meeting with our rival families in the first place, so I could establish my authority.

Yet, I'd assumed the position was temporary. Nothing I did mattered because everything would eventually go back to the way it was.

Not now.

Nothing in my life would be the same now.

Thunder rumbled overhead and I jumped. The storm was blowing in faster than I thought.

Grabbing my hand and turning it palm up, Garrison studied the splitter sticking out of my thumb.

"All that and you still won't say the word." With one quick motion, he plucked the splinter free. "Please, tell me I'm wrong, Alex. Tell me it's all in my paranoid head and you're not actually involved with the mafia."

Blood dripped down my thumb and collected in the cup of my palm. Such a little splitter caused a lot more damage coming out than going in.

I shoved my hand in my pocket before more blood could fall.

"Not just *involved*. I'm its damn leader

now."

Garrison stared in silence, shocked by my answer.

Hypocrite.

I huffed, and a lock of hair fluttered away from my face. If Garrison couldn't accept the answer, then he shouldn't have asked.

More thunder crashed overhead, turning the sky into its personal percussion band.

Snapping out of his shock, Garrison slammed a fist into the railing hard enough to make the wood groan.

"Damn it, Alex. Why?" He stepped forward, crowding into my space.

I took a step back. "What'd you mean, why?"

"Why didn't you tell me?"

Anger sparked within me like the lightning still hiding in the clouds above.

How dare this man demand even more answers, forcing me to retreat like I was some soldier to be ordered around. I shoved at Garrison's chest, managing to put a little space between the two of us.

"I don't usually have to explain. As soon as people hear my name they know what's up. It's not my fault you're ignorant."

Garrison's hand flew into the air, gesturing haphazardly at the horizon. "I've been serving overseas for the last twenty years. Sorry I'm not up to date on the names of my local mafia."

Pain flashed across Garrison's face and his arm dropped to his side. He schooled his features back into righteous anger, but he couldn't hide the way he gripped his arm.

He was still injured from their fight at the aquarium. A dark stain slowly spread over his suit as blood seeped from the knife wound just above his elbow.

On instinct I reached for Garrison, but the other man pulled back.

Garrison sighed and his anger disappeared. Instead, the lines around his eyes deepened into a look of exhaustion.

"You assumed I recognized your name. I can accept that. But you must have eventually realized that I didn't know. That's the part I'm having trouble with."

Finally, Garrison abandoned his perfect posture and braced both hands against the railing. Blood from his wound dripped down his arm and smeared over the wood.

"The more I think about it, the more it doesn't make sense. Either you were stupid enough to think your identity wouldn't matter, or you thought I was stupid enough not to notice. And I know you're not stupid, so that only leaves one option."

My phone buzzed in my pocket. It was probably my mother wondering what was keeping me.

As subtly as I could, I hit the ignore button. I could only deal with one problem at a time.

If Garrison noticed the interruption, he didn't react. In fact, he barely seemed to see the marina laid out before us as he stared into the middle distance.

"Was it fun watching me make a fool of myself? I knew you weren't serious about me. Why would you be? But I thought I was at least a player in your game, not a pawn in it."

The phone buzzed again, and I didn't bother hiding it as I hit ignore. I was being pulled in too many different directions. I could barely hear myself think inside my own head.

"Shut up." I shoved Garrison hard enough to make the man stumble back a step. "I have too many things to worry about. I can't handle your judgment as well. Don't make assumptions about me. You don't know what I'm serious about. Now, get in the car. We'll finish this conversation once we're safely at the house."

I turned to head for the open car door still waiting for us, but after a few steps I realized Garrison hadn't followed.

The man stood with his head bowed, staring at the patch of sidewalk where I had just been standing.

"No."

I drifted back to Garrison's side. "What do you mean no? You can't just say no."

"I mean I'm not going with you. I need... I need to leave."

At the last moment, I remembered the wound on Garrison's arm and diverted my aim. Instead, I grabbed Garrison's wrist to tug him toward the car.

"You're my bodyguard. You can't just leave. Come on."

"No." Garrison easily pulled out of my grip. "You're certain that your mother isn't the one trying to kill you, right? Then you should be safe with her. I just... I need to think, and I can't do that around you."

Before I could stop him, he turned and walked away. Only a bloody handprint remained behind, staining the railing in the place where he once stood.

My phone buzzed again.

With a shout I threw the device into the water below, then stormed back to my car, climbed in, and pulled the door closed. The car took off as I sat back in the seat, my gaze focused out the window, carrying me to the other side of the bridge just as the storm finally hit and it started to rain.

CHAPTER TEN

Alex

A DROP OF wine slid down the rim of the glass and over my fingers. I sat in the middle of an elegant staircase with a half empty wine bottle at my side. There were more comfortable places to sit in the front room of my family's house, but that spot gave me the best view of the portrait hanging over the door.

Raising my glass, I toasted the painted image of my father.

"Long live the King. Killed by his own empire."

"Don't speak about the departed like that."

I had known Valente my whole life and easily recognized the man standing at the bottom of the stairs without even looking. Rather than respond right away, I first drained the rest of the wine in my glass.

"What? It's true isn't it? He went and got himself killed and left me with this mess to clean up. He's not even in his grave yet and he's probably rolling in it."

Looking at the empty glass, I considered pouring myself another drink, but it would take too much effort. Instead, I let the wine glass dangle by the stem from my fingers and watched the last drops of red fall to the floor.

"Maybe it's good that he died before he had to see me take over. This way he can't be disappointed."

A pair of spotless leather shoes stepped into my vision. As usual, Valente hadn't made a sound when he moved.

"I don't know what your father would think about you right now, but he would have supported you." In an odd show of emotion, Valente's mouth and eyes drew tight around the edges. He looked back at the portrait on the wall. "Being the head of the Mariano family doesn't leave room for soft emotions, but I know your father loved you in his own way. In fact, I think you're the only one he loved."

As much as I wanted to argue, I couldn't find a single word to say.

If anyone could claim they understood David Russo, it was Valente. The man who had stood beside my father since before I was born.

The relationship between my father and I had never been easy. I knew, in many ways, I wasn't the son my father wanted. I didn't blindly follow orders. I didn't commit myself to the role of the perfect heir. I didn't live, breathe, and die for the family.

Yet, I couldn't think of a time when my father truly didn't support me.

When I insisted they take in my cousin Ghita, who was only twelve at the time, to keep her out of her father's clutches, my father had agreed.

When I came out and turned down the marriage that had been set up for me, my father hadn't fought me about it or tried to make me hide my sexuality.

When I had insisted on enjoying my freedom and refused to get too tangled in the family's affairs, my father had given me that freedom.

I shook my head. If I went down that train of thought I'd end up questioning everything about my life, and I wasn't ready for that level of self-reflection.

Instead, I set my empty glass aside and climbed to my feet, adjusting the cuffs of my sleeves to hide the wobble in my balance. I hadn't bothered to read the label, just grabbed the first bottle of wine I found. It must have been a stronger vintage than I realized. I wasn't fully drunk yet, but I was more inebriated than expected.

"You've questioned the surviving assassins from the aquarium, right? Any updates on who tried to kill me."

When Valente looked away from the portrait and back toward me, his neutral expression was back to normal. "A little, yes. We suspect it may have been the Bianchi family."

I nearly missed a step as I descended the stairs, but this time I could blame it on surprise rather than alcohol. "Really? Of all the possibilities, I wouldn't have thought..."

I'd met the heads of two rival families during the meeting at the aquarium. The Bianchi family, and the Vidales family.

Between the two, I'd always been on better personal terms with the Bianchi family. Their leader, D'Angelo Bianchi, shared many of my same values.

Caprice Vidales, on the other hand, was a hard woman who could make enemies with a bat of her eyelashes. Her distain for me was as bold as the polish on her nails.

Especially, after I turned down the marriage to her niece.

I came to a stop at the bottom of the stairs. "You said you suspect the Bianchi family is behind it? So, you don't know for sure."

Valente gave only the barest nod of his head. "We haven't gotten a clear answer out of anyone yet. However, they've hinted that they'd be willing to trade information for safety, since their employer probably isn't happy with them. One man let slip that the person who hired them was at the aquarium and got shot in the crossfire."

I clearly remembered the head of the Bianchi family taking a bullet in the arm. I'd been half hidden behind a bench at the time, so I hadn't gotten a clear view, but the man's thick, dark hair was impossible to mistake.

"That's not enough. We need solid answers. My mother is with the survivors now, right?"

The main part of the house looked no different than any other residence in Mantoloking. Each grand building encroached on its neighbors without actually touching. The Mariano family's estate wasn't the largest in the area, though it came close.

Its true uniqueness was found in what lay below ground level.

The only word I had for it was a *dungeon*. Concrete walls were insulated to block out all sound, and plexiglass walls divided the area into separate cells. It ensured that prisoners could see each other, but not hear anything.

The physiological warfare it caused worked wonders. Often people would crack just from seeing what was happening to others, knowing it would soon happen to them. In that way, you could torture a dozen people simply by hurting one.

Several of the cells were currently filled, each holding one person strapped to a chair. Some only had minor injuries, while some were barely hanging on to life. One of the cells held a man I vaguely recognized. Not enough to know the man's name, but enough to know he worked for our family.

At least he did, until now.

The man in the cell was in the worst condition out of everyone. Stripped naked and castrated, both his hands and feet had been removed so his limbs ended in mangled stumps.

Watching the man for a moment, I realized I couldn't see any chest movement. The man was already dead, propped up on the chair like a child's doll.

Perhaps my mother had decided to keep the corpse on display as a message to the other prisoners.

I found her in a cell with another prisoner. She stood over the bound man with a pair of bloody pliers. Several of the man's teeth and fingernails already sat in a bowl on a nearby table. The interrogation had come to a halt as my mother decided what piece to remove next.

Yet, surprisingly, instead of cowering in fear, the prisoner was laughing.

"You think your family is untouchable,

but we came so close to killing your brat. Would have succeeded if not for that so-called bodyguard of his. We thought it was just another boy toy. He's had so many before. It was only bad luck that this one turned out to be a trained soldier."

At the word *toy* several images flashed through my brain at once.

A bridge with a bloody handprint.

Wine dripping down the wall, and a bent iron headboard.

Club lights casting a halo around Garrison when the man protected me the first time.

Lightning flashing as Garrison walked away.

The knife was in my hand before I realized what I was doing. I practically knelt on the chair over the bound man, pressing the tip of my knife between his grinning blood-spattered lips.

"Say that again."

The man didn't answer, unable to talk around the blade stabbing into his tongue.

Fury twisted my face until my lips pulled back over my teeth. I yanked the knife to the side, slicing through the side of the man's mouth.

"Come on. Say it again. Call him a *toy* again."

Bright crimson blood flowed like wet Jello from the man's open cheek. He babbled something, but the words were lost in the gore flowing down his chin and over his chest.

My vision blurred around the edges, coating the world in a red mist. I didn't feel the impact as I drove my knife into the man's throat over and over. I didn't smell the blood or hear the last gasp of air escape from dying lungs.

Harsh hands grabbed me and pulled me back.

"Alex." My mother shook me several times to get my attention. "Alex, get a hold of yourself."

I had just enough mental clarity to make sure the knife didn't cut my mother as I shoved her away. "Fucker deserved it." Blood dripped down the blade over my hand, my fingers sticking together with the gore.

My mother grabbed the knife from me and started cleaning the blade. "Of course he deserved it. He tried to kill you. But we can't get information out of a corpse. I taught you better self-control than that."

"I won't just stand here while that bastard spouts bullshit."

"He can spout whatever he wants. The more someone talks, the better. That's how we get information. You know all that." Once the knife was clean, she folded up the blade and handed it back to me. "You aren't yourself right now. I understand your father's death has come as a shock. Go rest. I'll take care of things here. Come back once you've calmed down."

I stared at the knife being offered to me. It was a familiar weapon. I'd carried it for years. Yet, at that moment I couldn't bear the touch of cold metal.

Turning away, I stormed out of the cell and up the steps until I was out of the basement all together, leaving the knife behind.

Back in the main body of the house, I returned to the front room where my family's portrait hung. The half empty wine bottle still waited for me on the stairs. Not bothering to find a glass, I brought the bottle to my lips and drained the rest of its contents.

The wine didn't last as long as I'd like.

Soon enough, my throat was dry again, and I was left clutching an empty bottle.

That was how my cousin, Ghita, found me. She stood a step above me, arms crossed as she studied me half draped over the stair railing.

"How much have you had to drink?"

I raised the bottle in my hand. "Just the one."

Grabbing me by the wrist, she tugged my arm over my shoulder. "I think it was more than that. I know you. This is not you after just one bottle."

I let myself be pulled away from the railing, but I immediately tripped over the next step. "Not myself. Mother said that too. Not myself."

Ghita nodded along as she guided me up the stairs, one difficult step at a time. "Aunt Serafina is usually right. You'll feel better after some rest."

The world spun with each step. Maybe I had drunk more than I realized. I tried to remember, but my thoughts were like water slipping through my fingers. They flowed in whichever direction they wanted.

"You're both wrong. I'm too much myself. That's why he left."

My unsteady balance tipped me hard to the side, and I nearly tumbled to the floor. Ghita barely managed to hang on to me long enough to set me down, then joined me sitting on a step just a few feet from the top of the stairs.

Her chest heaved and a drop of sweat rolled down her temple.

"Who left? You're not talking about your father, are you?"

"No." I leaned against the railing, tapping at the bottle I still held in one hand. "Garrison. My bodyguard. That's what you said, right? Get a bodyguard. Well, I did. Real interesting one."

Through a mix of disjointed sentences, I managed to recount the whole situation. It probably wasn't the best explanation, but it seemed to be enough as Ghita nodded along.

"So, you hired this Garrison guy because you thought he was attractive. Didn't tell him you're mafia. Slept with him. Then, when he found out the truth, he left."

"Hey..." I pointed at her with the neck of the bottle. "I hired him because he's a badass soldier who saved me. And because I wanted to climb him like a tree." A rush of heat warmed my cheeks and I giggled. "Seriously. I could have, too. Guy's got shoulders for days. Fucking him is like scaling Everest."

I gestured too wildly with the bottle and nearly fell over again.

Ghita grabbed me by the shoulders, pulling me back before I could somersault down the stairs. "I don't want to know about your sex life. But I am wondering... what did you think would happen?"

The world spun. I tried to ignore it and focus only on Ghita.

"What do you mean?"

With a groan, Ghita climbed to her feet and pulled me up as well.

"I mean, what was your end goal here? You knew he had to find out eventually. So, what was your plan?"

We managed to make it to the top of the stairs and started the long trek down the hall toward my room.

An unfamiliar carpet passed beneath my feet. My mother must have redecorated recently.

"No plan. I just wanted..." I trailed off, distracted by the carpet. The old pattern had been better.

We reached my room and Ghita

propped me against the wall so she could open the door. "I know. You just wanted to get him into bed."

"No." I shook my head so hard it hit the wall. "I wanted... He was *mine*."

The door swung open, but Ghita didn't pull me into the room. "What do you mean, he was yours?"

"I mean he was *mine*," I repeated again, louder this time. "Not employed by my family. Not provided by someone else. Just *mine*."

"Ah." Ghita nodded, and wrapped her arms around my waist. Propping her shoulder into my armpit, she guided me inside. "I think I see."

Well, at least one of us did, because I still felt clueless.

She helped me stumble over to the bed and pushed me down until I sat unsteadily on the mattress.

"Can you handle it from here? As much as I love you, I'm not undressing you."

I waved her off, assuring her that I could take care of myself. Although the words were more of a slurred mess than actual syllables.

She ran a hand over my hair. "Good.

Get some rest. We'll talk about this more in the morning once you sober up."

As she left, I waved the bottle at her. "I only had one."

The door clicked shut and I was alone.

I sat motionless on the edge of the bed. The whole room spun. Even the slightest twitch of my muscles sent me reeling.

Without moving my head, my vision blurry, I stared in confusion down at the bottle in my hand.

I'd only had one.

A feeling of dread descended on me like a curtain drawing across my vision.

Something was wrong. I knew my own alcohol tolerance. I shouldn't be this drunk from only one bottle.

I tried to stand up and go after Ghita, but my feet wouldn't hold my weight and I fell to the floor. My vision was really going dark.

The carpet pressed against my cheek as I lay on the floor, unable to move or even call out. My fingers went limp and the empty bottle rolled out of my hand.

Just before I passed out, I heard the door open again.

Then everything went black.

CHAPTER ELEVEN

Garrison

THREE DAYS AFTER the argument with Alex, I ran down a familiar path. I'd started the run an hour earlier than usual and my breath fogged in the frosty morning air. What little sun peeked over the horizon was mostly blocked by the trunks of the surrounding trees. The time could barely be called dawn when I stopped and sat on a park bench along the side of the trail.

Moments later, familiar uneven footsteps approached. Caden struggled over the gravel path. With his one good arm, he held the cane that kept him upright, while he tried to balance a container of coffee cups with his other arm in a sling.

"Why the hell did you want to meet out here?" Caden collapsed onto the bench, tossing his cane aside and shoving the coffee at me. "It's too damn early to walk all the way out here. Makes me feel like an old man hobbling around like this. Fuck, I'm not even forty yet. So, what's up? You better have a good reason for asking me to meet you here."

I hadn't asked Caden to bring coffee, but I appreciated it nonetheless. We divided up the cups, then both of us simultaneously leaned back against the bench with a groan.

Minutes passed, each of us taking sips of our drinks in silence before I started the conversation.

"You knew."

Caden didn't bother to respond, just gave an inquisitive hum around the paper rim of his cup and waited for me to continue.

"You knew that club was owned by the Italian mafia when you took me there to interview for a job. And based on your reaction when you saw him, you knew exactly who Alex Mariano was. Why didn't you tell me?"

It was cold enough that the steam from our coffee didn't last long. The drink had already cooled enough for Caden to chug the rest of his.

"To be honest, I thought you already knew. It wasn't until you accepted the job as his bodyguard that I realized you didn't, but what could I do about it then?"

"You could have warned me before even taking me to the club. Even if you assumed I would recognize the Mariano name, I couldn't have known who owned the club."

"Well..." Caden reached for his drink, only to remember at the last moment that it was empty. Instead, he fidgeted with the sling supporting his arm. "You needed the money, and the bouncer job was legit. Even if the Mariano family owns it, the place still needs to function as an actual club. So, you wouldn't need to get involved with anything illegal."

Half of my coffee still sat in the cup, but I set it aside anyway. "Then why did you pass on Alex's message to me?"

The look Caden gave me made me feel like my intelligence had suddenly been cut in half.

"I work for the club, so it was easiest for them to get in contact with you through me. And when the Mariano family personally asks you to do something, you don't tell them *no*. Not if you want to keep breathing." He grabbed my half full cup and downed it as well. "Bleh. Why don't you use sugar?" The newly empty cup joined his original cup in the trashcan next to the bench. "Look, Garrison, you're asking a lot of questions, but I don't think any of this is what you actually want to know. So why don't you ask your real question? It's too early for these kinds of games."

Caden's choice of words prickled under my skin. They were too close to the accusations I'd directed at Alex.

I wasn't playing games. I just didn't know how to ask what I wanted without it sounding like an insult.

"You work for that club, which means you work for the Italian mafia. So, I just want to know... how?"

The wind blew, bringing with it the first hints of daytime warmth, yet Caden's demeanor turned icy. "What kind of work do I do for them? Mostly, I'm just a courier. Don't need four working limbs to drive a vehicle, and my handicap license means I can park pretty much anywhere and no one will ask questions. So long as I don't get too curious about what I'm transporting, it's fine."

I wasn't sure if I should feel relieved or frustrated. It was good to know that Caden wasn't involved in anything too violent, but it didn't answer my question.

"No, I mean... how did you get your head around working for the mafia in the first place. You were a soldier. You worked for the military. How did you go from protecting people to hurting them?"

Caden jumped to his feet, nearly falling over when his bad leg refused to support his weight. "Hey, I don't hurt anyone. I just drive a truck."

He fumbled for a moment as he retrieved his cane from the ground, but he didn't leave. Instead, he stood with his back to the bench, staring off into the shadow of the trees.

"Ask yourself this, Garrison. Did we ever really protect people? We didn't serve together, but we were in similar units. If your service was anything like mine, then you probably had to hurt a lot of people and do a lot of things that would horrify the average civilian."

The scars on my back ached, and my knee jerked as old pains flared up again.

Caden turned back to face me, shuffling over the gravel to avoid losing his balance again. "It did bother me when I first accepted the job, but I realized that the mafia wasn't asking me to do anything that the military didn't demand. Less even. I'm not required to kill anyone now."

We'd been sitting around long enough for the sun to finally stretch its rays above the trees. Sunlight chased away the dew clinging to the grass and provided a promise of warmth.

I shook my head. "It can't be that easy."

"It's not easy," Caden agreed. "But neither was being a soldier. Think about it. What's really the difference between working for the military and working for the mafia? We end up doing the same thing, either way. If we kill someone, then they're dead. It doesn't matter who authorized us to pull the trigger. Dead is still dead. Violence is still violence. The only difference I can see between our old masters and our new ones, is that our old masters had the authority to declare our crimes legal. Our new masters don't."

I had specifically chosen this bench because it was nowhere near the playground at the front of the park. Yet, at that moment I swore I could hear the sounds of children screaming in my ears. I wanted to cover my head and block out the noise, but it wouldn't help. The park was silent. There was no hiding from the horror-filled contents of my own mind.

A flash of sunlight glinting off metal broke me away from my memories. I dived off the bench and knocked Caden aside. We both skidded over the gravel, but I was immediately on my feet. A knife stuck out of the bench, right where I had been sitting.

One of the stitches on my arm popped open. A drop of blood ran over my skin, but I barely noticed as I followed the knife's trajectory back to the person who had thrown it.

"Impressive." A short, curvy woman with an even shorter haircut stepped out from the shadow of a tree. "Alex said you were good. Seems he was right."

Without looking away from the woman,

I helped Caden clamber back to his feet.

"Who are you?"

The woman came to a stop well outside my reach. She looked relaxed, but she was obviously still wary of me.

"I'm Ghita Mariano. Alex's cousin."

The name was familiar. Alex had mentioned his cousin a few times, but I couldn't remember much about the woman. I certainly couldn't think of a reason for her to be there now.

"Did Alex send you? I told him, I need some time to think. I'll contact him when I'm ready to talk."

Right before my eyes, Ghita's confidence seemed to deflate. "So, he's not with you?"

"What? No. Why would he be with me? I specifically asked for time away from him."

She pressed her hands against her mouth like she was praying. "I thought... or at least I hoped that he'd just left to fix things with you. If not, then..."

She squeezed her eyes shut, but a few tears snuck free.

After pulling the knife from the bench and returning it to her, I guided Ghita to take a seat. "Deep breaths. Just like that.

Now, tell me what's going on."

She wiped her eyes, smudging mascara across her lower lids. "Alex is missing. I was hoping he'd just left, but now I think he was taken."

The sound of her words, so absolute in their meaning, shot fear through my heart. My whole body seemed to go numb, and my vision tunneled. At that moment, my whole world consisted only of the woman sitting on the bench.

I grabbed her shoulders and barely stopped myself from shaking her. "What happened? Who took him? I thought he was staying with his mother."

Before Ghita could answer, Caden pulled me away from the bench. "What are you doing? I thought you didn't want to get involved with the Mariano family anymore."

I nearly shoved Caden away, until I remembered at the last moment to curb my strength. Instead, I merely patted the man's shoulder.

"I said I wasn't sure. I haven't made any decisions yet. But none of that matters right now if Alex is missing."

Taking a deep breath, I sat beside Ghita on the bench and stretched out my aching leg.

"Tell me everything that happened."

She gave as clear an explanation as she could while also holding back tears. From interrogating the surviving assassins, to their suspicions about the Bianchi family. She even described Alex getting drunk and how she helped him into bed.

"When I went to check on him later, the room was empty. No one could find him anywhere. It's like he just... vanished."

With a grunt of effort, Caden sat on Ghita's other side. He didn't seem happy to be there. Rather, he had the air of one resigned to their fate. "And you're sure he didn't leave on his own?"

"That's what Aunt Serafina and Valente are saying. He's been visibly upset since his father's death, and they think the pressure of taking over the family got to him. But, I've known Alex my whole life. He wouldn't just leave. And... I keep thinking about something he said right before he disappeared. He was super drunk when I helped him to his room. It didn't seem strange then, but he insisted that he only drank one bottle of wine.

That's enough to get him tipsy, but not enough to leave him stumbling around like he was."

It didn't take much for me to pick up what she was implying.

"You think he was drugged."

"Maybe. I don't know." From a purse draped over her shoulder, she pulled out an empty wine bottle. It was sealed in a Ziplock bag like a prop on a detective show. "Hopefully, this will give us some answers."

I took it from her and studied the bottle without opening the bag. Nothing looked out of place, but drug residue wouldn't be visible to the naked eye.

"Have you told your family about this?"

"No." Ghita snatched the bottle back and hid it in her purse. "If someone was able to abduct Alex right from his own bedroom without getting caught, that means they're able to walk around the house without being noticed. One of our own men turned out to be an assassin at the aquarium. We thought they were the only traitor, but if there are more, then I don't know who to trust. That's why I came to you."

"Me?" I looked up in surprise. "Why

me?"

She shrugged. "Because Alex trusted you. Besides, you're too inexperienced with all this to be a traitor. From what Alex said, you didn't even know he was mafia until a few days ago. So, will you help me find him?"

It should have been a hard decision.

Alex had just inherited the title of *Mafia Boss.*

Alex had lied to me.

Alex probably never wanted to see me again after our fight on the bridge.

Yet, from the moment I heard Alex was in trouble, I could only give one answer.

"Yeah. All right. I'll help you."

Surprisingly, it was Caden who reacted first. Leaning heavily on his cane, he stood from the bench and stretched his good arm over his head until his back popped.

"Well, come on. If we're gonna find your boyfriend, we'll need to start by getting that bottle tested. I know someone who can help."

I scowled and stared at Caden in confusion. "Boyfriend? Who said anything about..."

Caden cut me off before I could finish.

"Oh, please, you aren't subtle. Constantly referring to him as *Alex*. Freaking out the moment you hear he's in trouble. It wasn't hard to figure out."

Ghita giggled and followed Caden down the gravel path. "Doesn't take any bullshit, does he? I like him. Come on, Garrison. Let's go save my idiot cousin so the two of you can kiss and make up."

CHAPTER TWELVE

Garrison

MY KNEES KNOCKED against the car's front dash and my elbow pressed uncomfortably into the armrest. The car wasn't big enough for me, but it had been the only one available at the rental agency on such short notice. We hadn't wanted to waste time shopping around, so I'd resigned myself to squeezing into the small space.

At least I didn't have to drive. Ghita sat behind the wheel, navigating the car that was perfectly proportioned to her size.

We'd started driving before we even knew where we were going. As we waited for Caden's contact to get back to us with answers about the wine bottle, we decided to visit one of Ghita's informants that kept track of the Bianchi family for her.

We were nearly at the New Jersey border when we finally got a call from Caden with results. To no one's surprise, Alex's wine bottle had been laced. I didn't ask too many questions about Caden's contact who'd tested the bottle for us. The less I knew about it, the better. All I cared about were answers.

"What the hell is this?" I said as I looked at the information scrolling across my phone. I'd never gone to college—I'd worked minimum wage jobs for a few years then said *fuck it* and joined the military when I was twenty-one—and the info on the paper didn't resemble anything from my high school chemistry class.

"I don't know," Caden's voice spoke through the phone's speaker. "My contact has never seen this drug before. Couldn't tell me anything about it."

Pulling the car over to the side of the road, Ghita grabbed the phone out of my hand. She barely had to glance at the screen.

"It's called Vibe. It was supposed to be a less addictive alternative to alcohol, but too large of a dose can knock a person out for days."

I may not know much about drugs, but even I could tell something was amiss. "That seems like a strange choice of drug to kidnap someone. Chloroform would work just as well."

"Perhaps," Ghita nodded as she handed back the phone. "But it does confirm one thing. Wanna guess who invented Vibe and controls the only supply?"

"The Bianchi family?"

With a squeal of tires and revving gears, Ghita pulled the car back onto the road. "Give the man a prize. Yep. They must be involved somehow. With any luck, they'll lead us to Alex."

We flew down the highway, heading toward the northern part of New York. As much as I wanted to storm right into the Bianchi family's home and demand Alex back, I knew that wasn't the right move. We needed to be smart about this, and charging right into our enemy's hands would only get us killed.

First, we needed information, and that

was apparently Ghita's specialty. She had informants strung along the east coast that kept tabs on various powerful families for her. So, that's where we were headed, to one of her informants who specifically watched the Bianchi family. Although it would take a few hours to get there.

I hated long car trips. They gave me too much time to think. Staring out the window, cramped in a too small seat, my thoughts wandered.

The Bianchi family had plenty of influence back in Italy. It was what made them such a powerful rival to Alex's family. If they'd taken Alex overseas, it would be nearly impossible to find him. I would not only have failed as a bodyguard, but I would never see the other man again.

That thought hurt worse than I expected, and I'd known plenty of pain in my life.

No, I had to hold on to the hope that Alex was still alive and somewhere nearby. I would find him, and we'd talk. Properly this time, without fighting. Even if it resulted in the two of us parting ways for good, I would still rest easy knowing

Alex was safe without me.

The hours in that car passed so slowly, I would swear the clock was moving backward. I wasn't normally a claustrophobic person, but I was going stir crazy in that little car with nothing to do but fret.

When Ghita finally brought the car to a stop, announcing we'd arrived, I was out the door before the wheels even stopped rolling. The building that stood before me was the most average looking apartment complex I'd ever seen. Even as I stared at it, I couldn't pick out a single noteworthy detail. Yet somewhere, within that boring maze of beige squares, Ghita's informant hid in plain sight.

An "Out of Order" sign hung on the elevator, so we climbed the stairs up to the third floor. Rows of identical doors were differentiated only by the numbers hanging on plaques beside each frame. Ghita knocked on the very middle door.

"Hey, Jason. It's me. Your sister. The post office sent me your mail again."

She shook her head when I flashed her a questioning look. I assumed it was some sort of code they'd worked out between them.

No answer. Ghita knocked again, and again received only silence.

"That's not good. He always answers."

Instinct tingled along the back of my neck. I tried the doorknob, and to my dismay it opened.

Definitely not good.

Pulling the gun from my hip, I told Ghita to step back and pushed the door open.

In the middle of an average looking living room, a man lay tied up on the floor. I assumed this was Jason. I had just enough time to notice that the man was alive before focusing on the other person in the room.

A man with olive skin and dark hair sat in a chair facing the door, idly twirling a butterfly knife between his fingers.

I instantly recognized him from the meeting at the aquarium.

D'Angelo Bianchi.

Upon seeing me, the Bianchi family head smiled and leaned forward so his elbows braced against his knees.

"Finally. Took you long enough."

CHAPTER THIRTEEN

Alex

THE BED KEPT moving. I shifted, trying to find a spot on the mattress that would behave.

Something caused the whole bed to jolt, knocking me into consciousness.

I wasn't on a bed. I was sprawled on the floor of some sort of moving vehicle. Thick ropes secured my hands and feet so I could only raise my head by squirming around like a worm.

The windows of the vehicle were blacked out. I couldn't even tell the time of day.

My head spun and I lay still again,

willing myself not to throw up.

What had happened?

I remembered being back at the house in Mantoloking, helping my mother interrogate our prisoners.

Well, *help* was probably the wrong word. She interrogated. I just stabbed the person until they stopped talking.

Then I'd gotten drunk and Ghita helped me to my room.

Right?

I didn't remember drinking that much, but it would explain the pounding headache.

I had no idea what happened after I'd passed out, but I somehow ended up getting kidnapped. I wasn't even all that surprised. I certainly had enough enemies who would want to harm me. It was simply a matter of who had succeeded.

There was no telling how long I lay there, waiting for my head to stop spinning. It never did. With each bump in the road, my world was sent spinning again.

Definitely not just drunk, then. A hangover would usually abate over time.

Drugged maybe.

That would explain a few things,

though it also raised a lot more questions.

I wasn't sure if it was the drugs, or just the expectation that something like this would happen to me some day, but I felt surprisingly calm.

Too calm.

I was probably in shock, but even that thought didn't inspire more than passing interest. My thoughts were like a checklist running through my head.

Necessary steps for escape: number one, find a way to untie myself.

The back of the van was completely empty, and I'd been stripped of my weapons.

Unless...

Curling my spine as far as it would go, I managed to catch a glimpse of my own waist. They hadn't removed my belt. There was a hidden blade inside the buckle that I could use to free myself.

Unfortunately, my hands were tied behind my back, while the buckle was in front. When I was younger, I could have passed my hands around my feet to bring them in front. It was my favorite trick to pull whenever my father insisted on *training* me for these kinds of situations. However, I hadn't been that limber since puberty. If I tried now, I'd just end up dislocating my shoulders and I still wouldn't be free.

I arched my back to raise my head again, getting a better look at my surroundings. It was some sort of industrial van. Whoever was driving sat in a separate compartment up front. The back was meant for transporting goods and equipment, so it lacked seats and upholstery like a typical vehicle. This meant the metal structure lay completely exposed.

I squirmed over the floor until I found a spot in the van where two pieces of metal had been joined. A row of large bolts stuck up from the flat surface. I aligned my belt buckle with one of these bolts and used the edge to try and coax the hidden knife free.

It felt like I was humping the floor. If anyone saw me right now, they would probably die of laughter.

My spinning vision didn't help, either. I kept misjudging the alignment or moving too quickly and my buckle would slip free from the bolt with a ring of metal against metal. Each time that happened, I'd lie still for a moment to make sure I hadn't been noticed.

Luckily, whoever was driving the van wasn't paying me any attention. No one ever checked on me, not even when the van took a hard turn and I went rolling into the far wall.

Finally, with a thrill of victory, I managed to pull the hidden knife free from my buckle. It was only about two inches long and roughly shaped like an arrowhead, but the edge was sharp and would cut through the ropes binding me.

If only I could get it into my hands.

That required more squirming as I tried to position my hands where I thought the knife lay. Then, when my fingers touched nothing but cold floor, I scooted over an inch and tried again.

I found the knife by slicing my finger on the tip, but I didn't care about the pain. It was barely more than a paper cut, and I finally had the weapon in my hand.

Closing my eyes, I counted my breaths and got to work sawing at the ropes. They were thick and the knife was small, but one by one, I felt the fibers snap.

The rumbling vibrations beneath me fell silent.

The car had come to a stop. It was too

late. We'd arrived wherever my kidnappers were taking me, and my hands were still bound.

I had a choice to make. Try to free myself before anyone came for me, or pretend to be unconscious. If it was just my hands, I might have tried to escape, but my feet were bound too. I'd never cut through both in time.

Voices spoke just outside the van doors, arguing about something.

I made my decision and slumped over on the floor. I palmed the knife and gripped the rope around my wrists to hide the cut section.

The doors opened, and despite how much I wanted to see the identities of my kidnappers, I kept my eyes closed.

"We sure this is a good idea?" one of the kidnappers asked as they jumped up into the van beside me.

"These are the orders. Come on. Get his head."

At least two sets of hands grabbed me. Possibly three. I remained limp as a ragdoll, letting my head loll about on my shoulders.

They carried me for a while before throwing me unceremoniously to the ground. My head cracked against the concrete floor and stars danced behind my eyes. It almost distracted me from the pain of my secret knife stabbing into my palm. My first instinct was to let go, but I held on to the blade and prayed my kidnappers wouldn't notice the blood.

Another voice spoke from at least a few feet away. "What's the point of all this? Why not just kill the bastard and be done with it?"

"Those weren't the orders. Boss-man wants it done this way. So, we do it this way."

None of the voices sounded close, and the footsteps of my kidnappers seemed to be growing farther away. I took a chance and cracked one eye open just enough to take a look around.

I was lying on the floor of a construction site, surrounded by half-finished concrete and exposed rebar. All of my kidnappers stood gathered around a large metal container on the other side of the room. None of them were looking in my direction.

It only took a few more passes of the knife to finish sawing through the ropes on my wrists. Then, as quietly as I could and without sitting up, I curled into a ball to reach my ankles. Instead of trying to cut the ropes this time, I used the point of my knife to pick apart the knot holding it together. Blood flowed from the cut on my hand, making my grip slippery, but I managed to get it untied after only a few tries.

I didn't give my captors any warning. Just jumped to my feet and started running. They shouted after me as I blindly bolted for the nearest doorway.

While I'd been lying on the floor, the dizziness hadn't been too bad. The moment I started moving, however, everything seemed to turn sideways. It felt like I was trying to cross the deck of a ship during a hurricane. The floor kept tipping in different directions.

My shoulder slammed into the side of the doorway.

I fell into a wall.

My palm left a bloody smear across the surface as I pushed off the wall and kept running.

Everything was a blur. Loose beams and debris lay around the half-constructed building, threatening to trip me at every turn.

COURTING DANGER

Fresh air suddenly filled my lungs, clearing my head for a moment. I'd stumbled into an open area where the building's foundation hadn't been poured yet. Construction equipment sat around, waiting for the next job, yet there was no obvious exit out of this concrete maze.

I checked over my shoulder. My pursuers were out of sight, but judging by the sound of their voices, just around the corner. I took the opportunity to dive under the tire of a bulldozer. As I lay panting in the dirt, several sets of footsteps ran past my hiding place without noticing me.

Breathing a sigh of relief, I pressed my back against the massive tire and buried my face into my hands.

The numb shock that had kept me calm until that moment was wearing off. A shiver started in my chest and spread until even the tips of my hair seemed to tremble.

I wanted to go home. I wanted to see my mother and Ghita again. I wanted to attend my father's funeral and even take over my new responsibilities running the family.

I wanted Garrison.

We hadn't actually known each other long, but even in such a short amount of time Garrison had already become a symbol of safety.

I didn't have a lot of safety in my life.

But would Garrison even want to see me again?

The last time we'd been together, we'd fought. For good reason. I'd lied to the man, after all. Many people wouldn't be able to forgive such a thing.

No, I refused to die when our last interaction was so unpleasant. I was going to get out of this, I was going to find Garrison, and I was going to apologize. Even if Garrison didn't forgive me, at least my conscience would be clear.

Shaking off the panic that burned like molten copper in the back of my throat, I peered around the tire. It was night, and eerie shadows covered the construction site. The only light came from an advertisement billboard lit up with spotlights from below.

Whitelock Holdings.

I read over the name several times, sounding it out under my breath. It sounded familiar, but the memory was hard to find in the scattered chaos that my mind had become.

Whitelock Holdings?

Wasn't that the name of a company owned by the Bianchi family?

Now that I thought about it, I remembered my mother calling me with the news of the Bianchi family's latest enterprise. I hadn't been paying much attention at the time. My latest conquest had been kneeling at my feet sucking me off when the ring of my phone interrupted us, and I'd only been focused on hanging up as quickly as I could without seeming rude.

Still, I remembered the name. The company definitely belonged to the Bianchi family, which meant the construction site belonged to them as well.

Fuck.

Apparently, Valente was right. The Bianchi family were the ones trying to kill me.

I hadn't believed it at first. The assassins from the aquarium claiming they shot their own employer had seemed like flimsy evidence. Not enough for me to make any accusations.

This, however, was much more

damning.

Of all the possible suspects behind the attack on my life, the Bianchi family had been low on the list. I'd always gotten along with D'Angelo, but friendly acquaintances meant nothing between power hungry families.

That was one question solved. Now I just needed to survive long enough to do something about it.

Since my pursuers ran past, no one else had approached my hiding spot. This section of the construction site seemed empty. Even the noise of the city sounded distant.

What city was I even in?

It wasn't anywhere in New Jersey.

Something else to figure out once I was safe.

Slipping out from under the bulldozer, I crept as quietly as I could toward the billboard. Advertisements like that were usually displayed on the front of construction sites so more people could see them. That meant the way out of the site had to be somewhere nearby.

Just as I passed a stack of plastic piping, I felt a prick in the side of my neck. My hand shot up, as I expected to slap away a mosquito. Instead, I pulled away a small dart.

"Fuck."

The word barely left my mouth before my legs collapsed. I grabbed onto the stack of pipes, sending them clattering over the ground. It was no use. I couldn't even see straight enough to know which way was forward.

Footsteps approached and hands grabbed my shoulders.

"That was too fuckin' close," someone grumbled as my hands were secured with more rope. "You fuckers need to pay attention."

The man tying my feet paused mid-motion to argue. "Hey, don't look at me. You said he'd be unconscious for at least another day."

I kicked out at the man by my feet. "Let go." I managed to strike the man's shoulder, but the blow was barely hard enough to bruise.

For my effort, I earned a backhand across the face.

"Stop struggling, ya bastard."

I had no choice but to comply. Whatever they'd drugged me with had already seized control of my muscles. I could barely keep my head off the ground, let alone raise my hands enough to fight back.

Trussed up even tighter than before, I was hauled off somewhere. My vision kept fading in and out, so I couldn't tell if it was the same room or not.

This time, they didn't bother to leave me on the floor. They carried me over to a large metal container and dropped me inside. A lid immediately covered the open top, trapping me in darkness.

In the small confines of the container, my harsh breathing sounded like a freight train. I flailed my bound fists, banging against the sides of my new prison, but it was useless. The metal was unforgiving and didn't even dent.

The whole container shifted, and I was thrown against one wall. Just as I managed to right myself, it shifted again, tossing me in the other direction.

What was happening?

Were they moving me somewhere else?

The container tipped back and forth a few more times, before suddenly dropping. I hit the lid, then bounced off the floor, the impact knocking the air from my lungs.

COURTING DANGER

I lay there, confused and disoriented as I gasped for breath. Everything was dark, but I couldn't tell if that was from the container, or if my vision had failed. My confused thoughts slipped through my mind, haze around the edges like old photographs faded from time.

In my delirium, I thought I heard a soft sound like rain on a tin roof. It was almost soothing, until I realized what the sound meant.

The answer hit me with the force of a baseball bat to the chest.

I was being buried.

I pressed my hands against the lid of the container, desperately scratching at the metal with blunt fingernails.

The drug in my system kept me weak but wasn't enough to knock me fully unconscious. It was a last act of cruelty on my murderers' part. I had no choice but to listen as inch by inch my coffin was covered in what sounded like wet concrete.

Through all this, only one thought filled my head.

I was going to die, and I'd never get to apologize.

CHAPTER FOURTEEN

Garrison

I INCHED INTO the room, placing myself
between D'Angelo Bianchi and the door
where Ghita hid just out of sight in the
hall. I trusted her to protect herself. After
all, I'd seen the way she handled a knife.
However, a good bodyguard was always a
bodyguard, and the urge to put myself
between others and danger would always
win in the end.

Except, the Bianchi family leader
wasn't presenting as much of a threat as I
expected. The man never even looked up,
too busy fiddling with something on his
phone. He waved the device around for a

moment then scowled at whatever the screen showed.

As I debated what to do, Ghita leaned around the doorframe and spotted her informant unconscious on the floor.

"Jason, what... You bastard."

Finally, the Bianchi leader looked up and tapped Ghita's informant with the toe of his shoe. "Oh, please, you can't be mad when you were using this man to spy on me. What were you expecting to happen?" His eyes never strayed from us, but at the same time, he also pulled out a small notepad from the inner pocket of his jacket and started writing.

There was an arrogant lilt to the man's voice, like he knew he was the one in control despite being outnumbered. Any ideas I had of trying to fight the man head on went out the window. This was the type of person who wouldn't reveal his knife until it was sticking out of his enemy's neck.

Metaphorically, at least.

The man's actual knife was on open display in a sheath strapped to his leg.

Instead, I tried a tactful approach. Maybe there was a way for us all to leave this interaction alive. "If you knew this man was a Mariano spy, why come here yourself?"

The Bianchi leader shrugged. "After I heard that Alex had gone missing, I knew you'd show up here. I have business to take care of with the Mariano family." He pulled down one side of his jacket to reveal the bandage wrapped around his arm.

Then he held up the notepad so Ghita and I could read what he'd written.

I'm bugged. My family is overprotective. But it only transmits audio. Keep talking like normal.

Once he was certain his message had been read, he pulled back the notepad and started writing again.

"The new head of your family asked to meet with me, and in the process, I was shot. Now, you're claiming that it was a hit against Alex, but since I'm the one who was injured and he came out unscathed, I'm not so sure."

He held up the notepad again.

I'm being framed. I had nothing to do with Alex's disappearance.

Then he set another notepad on the table beside an empty chair.

"However, I'm willing to hear out

whatever apology you can scrape together. Maybe it'll change my mind."

Picking up the hint, Ghita claimed the open seat. As she started writing on the notepad, I moved to stand behind her so I could follow both the spoken and unspoken conversations.

Unlike the Bianchi leader, Ghita waited until she finished writing to speak again.

"It's just like we said. Someone was trying to kill Alex. I'm sorry you got caught in the crossfire, but it wasn't intentional."

Why sneak around like this?

If you didn't kidnap Alex, just say so.

The Bianchi family leader lounged in his own chair, pulling his jacket back over his wounded arm while also continuing to write.

"So you claim, but I have my doubts. Alex is new to his position. Taking out the leader of a rival family would be a good way to establish authority."

Many people in my family want Alex dead.

Losing him so soon after losing David would cripple the Mariano family, and we could take advantage of that.

If it gets out that I helped you, my position would be in jeopardy.

Just by looking over her shoulder, I could tell Ghita struggled to keep track of two conversations at once. I pulled the notepad from her hand and started writing, leaving her to handle the spoken conversation.

"We didn't arrange an attack on you. Believe it or not. It doesn't matter. However, you're right that Alex is missing. If you had anything to do with that, I promise, you will regret it."

As soon as she finished speaking, I flipped over the notepad for the Bianchi leader to read.

Why should we trust you?

All the evidence we have so far points toward you kidnapping Alex.

This made the Bianchi leader smirk and huff under his breath like he wanted to laugh, but he kept himself under control and played it off like a sneer.

"Sounds like dear Alex has made too many enemies. Not a good sign, considering how short a time he's had the position. Maybe the Mariano family should step down and let more... *capable* families handle things."

I'm not stupid enough to kidnap someone with a drug only my family controls.

Your real enemy is using me to cover their tracks.

A fair point.

The moment I'd heard about the Vibe drug in Alex's wine, I found it suspicious. It was an unusual choice of drug just to knock someone out. There were plenty of better solutions.

No, the drug had been used specifically to incriminate the Bianchi family.

But why?

Was it an attack against D'Angelo Bianchi, or had the man simply been a convenient scapegoat?

Ghita's fist slammed into the arm of her chair. "You mean we should just give in to you. I swear, if you've done anything to Alex, I'll—"

The Bianchi leader cut her off. "You'll what? Whether or not I'm involved, there's nothing you can do about it. So, go home, and maybe start preparing for a double funeral. It sounds like your cousin is going to end up six feet under, one way or another."

The Bianchi leader's eyes flickered

toward me with a pointed look.

There were paragraphs hidden in those blue depths that I couldn't translate, but I did know one thing. We needed to wrap this conversation up.

I quickly scribbled down a simple question.

If you're offering help, that means you have help to offer.

What is it?

Taking a moment to collect himself, the Bianchi leader stood and smoothed the wrinkles from his coat. In the same motion, he pulled an envelope from his pocket.

"I'm giving you one warning. Leave this city in the next five hours, or I can promise you'll not leave at all."

He placed the envelope on the table before striding from the room with a swish of his long coat. On his way out, he flashed the notepad one last time.

I hope you find him.

Alex actually seems tolerable.

I'd hate to lose him so soon.

Then he disappeared, shutting the door behind him so silently I never heard the click of the latch.

The moment he was gone, Ghita

scrambled for the envelope. Inside, she found a phone, a key, and a letter. Her hands trembled as she scanned the page, then she immediately turned her attention to the phone.

I picked up the letter when she was done.

I'm not sure who's trying to frame me for Alex's disappearance, or why, but I promise you my family had nothing to do with it. I know it must be hard to believe me since I'm one of the people who would benefit from the Mariano family's fall, but I have enough on my own plate right now. I don't need to adopt other family's problems.

As soon as I realized someone was trying to frame me, I started looking for anything else suspicious. My family has a property in this city, a construction site, that's been inactive for months. A few hours ago, the security cameras recorded movement on this property. This may or may not help, but I know I didn't authorize anything there.

The phone enclosed in this envelope has access to the security cameras of the construction site. It only includes the last twenty-four hours of footage, and connection will automatically cut off twenty-four hours from now.

Good luck. I sincerely hope you find him.

P.S. I've also included the key to a safe house outside the city, just in case you need it. No one should bother you there for a few days.

An address was handwritten into the bottom margin of the page. I assumed it was the location of the aforementioned safe house.

Hopefully, we wouldn't need to use it.

Folding up the letter and storing it, along with the key, in my pocket, I turned my attention to the phone in Ghita's hand.

"Anything useful on that?"

Ghita didn't look up and her fingers never stopped moving over the screen. "I haven't found any clear evidence of Alex on the security cameras. Most of the cameras are around the perimeter, not inside the site. However, a van did pull into the site a few hours ago. They might have transported him that way."

Breathing deeply, I instinctively moved my hand to my gun. "It's not a lot to go on, but it's all we've got right now. Let's

move quickly. That construction site is on
the other side of the city."

CHAPTER FIFTEEN

Garrison

AS GHITA AND I stared from an alley across the street at the construction site that D'Angelo Bianchi had mentioned, I withheld the urge to sigh again. Of all the missions I'd ever been on, this had to be the most disorganized of them all. I couldn't even call it a plan. It was more like a really ambitious hope masquerading as a plan.

We left the safety of the car and approached the construction site, sticking to the shadows as much as possible. It was late into the night, but there were plenty of spotlights around the entrance.

To avoid being seen, the two of us circled around the side of the area where a chain link fence stood hidden in the dark. Climbing it would make too much noise, especially since we had no way of knowing exactly how many people were inside. Instead, we would have to cut our way through.

Before coming here, we'd first raided the home of Ghita's informant for supplies. The man would eventually wake up in bed, missing a pair of bolt cutters, a package of water bottles, and several bathroom cleaners, but he would find a stack of cash in their place.

From the bag now slung over her shoulder, Ghita pulled out the bolt cutters and handed them to me. I cut a hole in the chain link fence just big enough for us to slip through. Once we were inside, I then rolled the damaged part of the fence back into place to hide the hole as much as possible.

"Now where?" I asked Ghita as I handed her back the bolt cutters.

She stored them back in the bag and consulted the phone that the Bianchi leader had given them.

"I'm not exactly sure where the van

stopped, but based on the security footage, I think it was headed somewhere beyond that building."

The building in question showed only the skeleton of architecture, with no walls or doors to speak of. Tools and equipment lay scattered around like they'd just been left one day and forgotten.

"All right, we'll head over there and keep an eye open for the van. Look for fresh tire tracks, or anything that's been recently disturbed."

We tried inching toward the left side of the construction site, but as we approached it became harder and harder to remain unseen. Unlike the front of the site, which was quiet as the dead, this area had plenty of life.

I couldn't get a good enough look to count the exact number of people, but it was too many to sneak past. I pressed Ghita behind a tractor and peered around the corner as I considered what to do.

The nearest person stood about a dozen yards away, with several spotlights illuminating the area. There was no way for me to cover the distance without being spotted. Even if I managed to knock that one out, I'd be gunned down by the other people nearby.

For the same reason, I couldn't just shoot the person. Until I knew how many enemies we faced, I couldn't risk bringing down an army on us.

A soft tug on my sleeve caught my attention. Looking back at Ghita, I found her pointing at something above us.

The scaffolding.

There was a low spot nearby where we could climb up. Then we could get a better look at our surroundings and the enemies we faced.

Between Ghita's short height and my bad knee, climbing the scaffolding proved challenging. It was a multi-step process. First, I would climb up, with Ghita supporting me. Then, she would hand me our bag of supplies before I pulled her up behind me.

It took us about twenty minutes to reach the building's second floor. It still didn't provide as much cover as I would prefer, but it was at least easier to walk around.

The layout of the building formed a 'U' around a central courtyard. The two of us followed this shape around the edge of the courtyard until we found an area where plywood had been nailed into a makeshift wall. It wouldn't stop a bullet, but it would at least block us from sight if any of our enemies happened to look up.

From here, I counted a dozen people scattered around the open courtyard. It wasn't an army, but it was more than Ghita and I could fight on our own.

"Over there." Ghita pointed at a bulldozer sitting almost directly below us. "The ground looks disturbed. Like someone was running."

She was right. Fresh footprints marked the dirt, with a pattern that suggested frantic movement. Even more odd, they disappeared right under the bulldozer.

"Stay here," I told her as I searched for a better way to climb down. "I'm going to go take a look."

I found a discarded ladder that looked like it hadn't been touched in months. Old wood and rusted joints creaked as I lowered it to the ground, the structure threatening to collapse under my weight.

My knee protested each time I stepped down another rung and I made sure to keep both hands securely on the ladder at all times.

As soon as my feet hit dirt, a spotlight

spun in my direction. I ducked behind the wheel of the bulldozer and held my breath. There was no way to avoid making noise on such a rickety ladder, but I'd been hoping it would be mistaken for ambient city sounds.

"You hear something?" someone said from just out of sight. Footsteps plodded across the ground, each one a little closer.

I crawled under the bulldozer just before someone stepped into sight. I pressed up against the back of the tire, hoping the equipment's shadow would be enough to conceal me.

Two people walked by, one of them absently pointing a flashlight into the darkest shadows of the night.

"Nah, I didn't hear anything. You're being paranoid."

"But I could have sworn I heard—"

"It's fine. We're almost done here. There's only about a half hour left before the bastard runs out of air. Then we can leave."

Runs out of air?

My heart rate doubled. There was no context where those words could mean anything good.

As the two people turned around to

head back, the flashlight's beam reached under the bulldozer. I curled tighter against the large wheel to stay out of sight, but as I did so, I noticed the light glint off something silver half-buried in the dirt.

It looked vaguely familiar.

As soon as the people with the flashlight left, I unearthed the silver object. A little silver ring sat innocently in my palm.

I had seen this ring before, hooked through Alex's eyebrow piercing.

Closing my hand into a fist around the ring, I bit my lip to keep from making a sound. Part of me had hoped they were wrong. That Alex was actually somewhere safe and this whole thing was a misunderstanding.

Now I knew for a fact that Alex was there and in danger.

Taking out my phone, I dialed Ghita's number. She answered before the first ring finished.

"Anything?"

I gave her a quick, whispered summary of what I'd found, including Alex's eyebrow ring.

She was silent for a moment with only

the sound of her harsh breathing to let me know the call was still connected.

When she finally spoke, her words trembled but her voice held strong.

"Right. So, we're on the right track. We just need to find him. I've been reviewing the security footage again. In one of the cameras, if you zoom in on the bottom corner, you can just see a taillight. I think it's the same one as the van. It's not far."

"Wait," I said quickly before she could hang up.

"What? If Alex is *running out of air*, then we need to move."

"Not yet. Finding him won't matter if we can't get him out. This is a good place for our plan. Let's take these guys out, then go find Alex."

I could hear her grinding her teeth against the need to argue.

"Fine," she snapped. "It'll take me a minute, so hold on. Do you have what you need?"

I searched my pockets and found the medical mask I'd procured earlier. One of the benefits of the recent pandemic, everyone had a few of those lying around.

"Got it."

"All right. In an open area like this, it

won't be enough to knock anyone out. Just disorient them."

With the mask secured over my mouth and nose, I flexed my hands and listened to the knuckles crack.

"That's all I need."

A minute passed. Then two. I kept an eye focused on the second floor and waited.

Impatience throbbed under my skin. I wanted to run off and find Alex just as much as Ghita did, but logic won out. This was the best course of action, no matter how badly it chaffed.

Finally, Ghita's silhouette peeked over the edge of the second floor. She tossed something into the air, which landed in the middle of the courtyard.

Several people shouted in surprise as they turned to see a water bottle rolling across the ground.

"What the hell?" someone said, tapping the bottle with their toe.

The liquid inside churned, and the bottle exploded. A thick gas billowed into the air, causing everyone in a ten-foot radius to gag and stumble around.

Several more water bottles rained down on the courtyard. Each one exploded upon impact, adding more gas to the air.

Apparently, one could make a rough chemical bomb by mixing the right substances together in a small container, like a water bottle, and sealing the top. Then just shake and throw.

I had dealt with homemade bombs before during my years of service, but never one this crude. It was barely ranked above a high school science project, but it worked. Everyone around the courtyard hacked and coughed, and those closest to the water bottles fell to their knees, disoriented.

Diving out from under the bulldozer, I ran for the nearest enemy. The medical mask helped, but it couldn't keep all the gas out of my lungs. Each breath burned, so I tried not to inhale too much. Fortunately, the construction site's open air diluted the gas enough so it wouldn't harm me.

Unfortunately, I had no way to cover my eyes. My vision started watering the moment the first water bottle exploded. I needed to end it and get out of the contaminated area as quickly as possible.

I moved between the gas clouds, darting from one person to the next and knocking them out with precise blows. A few people managed to fight back, swinging wild haymakers at me, or reaching for whatever weapon they could find. Those people I was less gentle with, slamming the butt of my gun into their temples to leave them slumped on the ground.

In just a few minutes, every enemy lay unconscious as the gas dissipated into the wind.

Ghita waved both her arms to get my attention from the second-floor scaffolding. "Great job," she shouted down. "Now, come on. The van is over this way."

We found the van parked at the edge of the construction site, on the opposite side from where we'd broken in. It sat behind a brick wall, almost completely hidden from view, with its back doors thrown wide open.

There was nothing else in the area except for a set of stairs leading down to a basement. I led the way down the stairs, gun at the ready in case we'd missed any enemies with our water bottle assault.

The room at the bottom of the stairs turned out to be a large storage area. It would probably become part of the building's foundation once construction was finished, but for now it was being used to hold spare supplies and bits of broken equipment.

It was also empty.

"No." Ghita pushed past me into the room, frantically looking around. "He has to be here."

I stashed my gun back in its holster. "Maybe he was here earlier. They could have moved him since then."

"But we're running out of time. Is there any clue where they might have taken him?"

She started searching through spare equipment, dumping bags on the ground and knocking over a stack of metal poles. Her shoe slid in a patch of wet cement, and she shouted in disgust. "What? Ugh. Why is the ground wet?"

"It's not wet." Kneeling near Ghita's feet, I touched his fingers to the cement. "It's freshly poured."

A thought occurred to me. Small at first, like a whisper in the back of my mind, it quickly took hold. An empty horror opened in the pit of my stomach and my hands trembled.

"Ghita, do you remember what D'Angelo Bianchi said? That *Alex would end up six feet under, one way or another?*"

I saw the moment she realized what I meant. Her eyes widened until the whites were visible all the way around the iris.

"No, they couldn't..." But she didn't even bother to finish that statement.

Yes, their enemies very well could.

I grabbed a pole from the pile Ghita had knocked over and stabbed the end down into the wet concrete. The pit was deeper than it seemed. The pole was taller than me, and half of it disappeared under the surface of the concrete before it hit the bottom.

Moving the pole around, I knocked against something hard. By tapping the pole like a blind man's cane, I felt out the shape of the object. It was some sort of square container, easily big enough to hold a person.

"Get more poles," I ordered Ghita as I wedged the one in my hand under the container.

The concrete pit was significantly

bigger than the container, providing enough room to slide the poles underneath. The container tipped and rolled as I used the poles to leverage one end off the bottom. Then, I repeated the process with the other side.

Inch by inch, we managed to raise the container higher until finally one end was completely uncovered. Heavy chains wrapped around the container, sealing it closed. As much as I hated the sight of them, I was also grateful. The chains were much easier to grip than the container would have been on its own. My back and knee screamed as I hauled the heavy metal container free from the pit, but I barely noticed. I was too busy desperately looking for any sign of life inside.

Together Ghita and I freed the chains with the bolt cutters and threw open the lid.

Alex lay inside, with his eyes tightly closed and his arms pinned down against his sides.

At first, the man didn't move. Despair gripped my heart when it seemed we'd come too late.

Then Alex's eyes shot open, and he sucked in big gulps of air. His chest heaved as he frantically looked around before his eyes met mine and our gazes locked together.

In a flurry of graceless limbs, Alex shot out of the container and threw himself at me.

The man's arms and legs wrapped around my torso, pinning me in place before Alex slammed our mouths together.

It was the most graceless kiss I had ever known, and also the most welcome.

CHAPTER SIXTEEN

Alex

WE KISSED UNTIL my already strained lungs screamed for air. I reluctantly pulled away just enough to take a few gasping breaths. As soon as I could breathe properly again, I intended to dive back in and continue the kiss, but I was distracted by the sound of Ghita clearing her throat.

She stood just a few feet away, silently raising an eyebrow at Alex's position in Garrison's arms.

Unashamed, I stared right back at her, making no move to get down or stand on my own feet. "What?"

"Oh, no." She rolled her wrist, gesturing like she was trying to wind time forward with her bare hand. "Please, carry on. We're not in the middle of enemy territory, or anything."

I responded by primly flipping her off, but I did climb down from Garrison's embrace. The ground seemed to shift under my feet as my balance failed me, and I clung to Garrison for support. Closing my eyes, I waited for the dizziness to pass.

"Come on." Garrison led me away from the open container that had almost become my coffin. "Let's get you out of here."

A hidden car waited for us a few blocks away. Ghita climbed behind the wheel while Garrison and I both slid into the back.

Without needing to ask, Ghita started the car and pulled out of the alley, obviously heading for a specific destination.

I didn't bother to ask where we were going, trusting that my cousin and Garrison had a plan. Instead, I slumped over to lay my head in Garrison's lap.

"Wake me up when we get there."

COURTING DANGER

It was a surprisingly short drive, not even enough time for a power nap. Just outside the city limits, we pulled into a shockingly average cottage. The only noteworthy feature was the amount of land it came with. Several acres of untamed trees surrounded the modest structure, hiding it from the world with a natural fortress of greenery.

When we stepped into the already furnished and well-stocked house, I revised my decision about questions.

"Okay, so, where are we? This isn't one of our properties."

Garrison tossed aside a bag filled with water bottles and cleaning supplies—they'd already explained about their homemade water bottle bombs—though he didn't remove his weapons. "This is apparently one of D'Angelo Bianchi's safe houses."

I paused. Certainly, I'd heard that wrong. "D'Angelo, the man who just tried to kill me?"

The plaid sofa cushions bounced when Ghita collapsed onto the furniture, exhaustion evident in every line of her body. "He claims it wasn't him. Said he was set up, though I'm not sure how much I believe that."

Garrison didn't sit. He remained on guard, standing just off to the side of the door and watching out the window.

"I think he was telling the truth. All the details of your kidnapping were too obvious. Dosed with a drug that only the Bianchi family controls. Taken to a property that the Bianchi family owns. If they actually did kidnap you, then they were going out of their way to incriminate themselves."

With her eyes closed and her head tipped back against the couch, Ghita shrugged. "I guess it does sound suspicious. And D'Angelo did help us out. At first, I thought it might be another trap, but he pointed us toward where you were being kept, and gave us access to this safe house."

Nodding along with what they were saying, I only half paid attention as he sidled closer to Garrison. "Guess I'll have to thank D'Angelo later."

Garrison turned away from the window, apparently satisfied that there was no danger lurking in the trees outside. "I wouldn't mention it. Apparently, the rest of the Bianchi family were eager for your death, even if they weren't the ones who did it. He had to help us secretly. Said something about already having enough of his own problems, he didn't need yours as well."

"Right. We can worry about that later. It's been a long... hours? Days? How long has it been since I was kidnapped? Whatever. Finding a bed sounds fantastic right now."

Half of Garrison's attention was still out the window, but luckily Ghita picked up on the odd tone in my voice. She glanced in my direction, her gaze flicking between me and Garrison, before heaving herself off the couch with more noise than necessary.

"This place seems to have several bedrooms. I'll be taking the one at the far end of the house, as far from you two as I can, and I don't expect to be bothered until morning."

Then she left the room, muttering under her breath about how it might actually be afternoon before anyone saw her.

Her departure left Garrison and I alone. The silence between us was nearly as smothering as the concrete I had been buried under.

"So..." Garrison shifted so his already immaculate posture stood a little straighter. "We should probably talk."

"Yeah, we should," I agreed, stepping closer to the man. "After."

"After?"

Before Garrison could say any more, I grabbed the front of his jacket and kissed him. It was sloppy, uncoordinated, and the best thing I had ever felt. Inside that container, frigid panic had hollowed out my chest. Even once I'd been saved, that emptiness remained. I tried to remain calm, cutting off the many emotions that threatened to spill out of the hole that panic had chewed through me.

The heat of Garrison's body pressing against mine filled that emptiness, but it wasn't enough. I needed more.

When Garrison pushed me away, I whined low in the back of my throat. The only thing that stopped me from losing my mind completely was the feeling of Garrison's hands still gripping my shoulders.

"Come on. Please." I tried to pull Garrison closer.

"This isn't a good idea. We fought the

last time we spoke. Then all this happened. We just... We should talk before anything else."

Right. Our fight.

I had almost forgotten.

I grasped Garrison's collar so tight some of the stitches popped. "I'm sorry. It was my fault. I should have told you the truth about my family sooner. And I promise we will talk about everything. Just... please." I pressed my forehead against Garrison's chest, feeling the rise and fall of the man's breathing. "I thought I was going to die. It still feels like that. Like part of me is still buried. I just need you to help me feel alive again. Then we'll talk about anything you want."

Even without looking up, I could feel the weight of Garrison's gaze on me. Silence persisted between us. It lasted so long, I was certain Garrison would reject me. The part of my brain that wasn't flooded with need and arousal wondered if it would be better for both of us if Garrison turned away from me right now.

However, that was a very small part. Mostly I just wanted to scream.

Still without saying a word, Garrison ran both hands down my side. Heat flushed through my system, making me moan, then gasp when those hands gripped my hips. I knew I wasn't a light person. Yet, Garrison barely seemed to struggle as he picked me up, guided my legs around his waist, and walked off toward one of the bedrooms.

To be carried so easily, it made me feel small in the very best way. Like I was something tender and precious, and I had the strongest protector shielding me from the rest of the world.

Muscles shifted and Garrison's body rubbed up against mine with each step that Garrison took. Arousal buried its roots in my gut, and I let myself be carried, clinging to the other man as I pressed kisses to whatever path of skin I could find.

We barely made it into the bedroom. As soon as the door closed behind us, Garrison pressed me against the wall. Our hips ground together, creating more pleasant friction that sent shivers through both of us.

Garrison stopped for a moment, a serious look on his face. "We're talking after this."

I nodded eagerly. At this point, I

probably would have agreed to anything Garrison said.

Yet, Garrison said nothing else. His mouth was too occupied, kissing me again and letting the long lines of our bodies drag against each other.

I kicked my feet in midair as I squeezed Garrison's hips with my thighs. This position should have left me feeling powerless. I couldn't do anything but let Garrison hold me up and trust that he wouldn't drop me.

Instead, it brought a sense of safety. Nothing could touch me when such a strong wall of muscle and bone surrounded me.

I suddenly snapped back to reality when Garrison set me down on my own feet.

"This house is pretty well stocked. The bathroom should have something. Get undressed while I fetch what we need."

He left before I could ask what he meant.

Still lost in a haze of arousal, and other less pleasant emotions I didn't want to think about, my legs shook with the effort of holding myself up. I slid down the wall until I was sitting on the carpet. It wasn't as cold on the floor as it was standing by myself, and I curled my knees closer to my chest as I waited for Garrison to return.

It wasn't a long wait, but every second that passed left me feeling a little colder. I sighed in relief when Garrison stepped into view. Even just the sight of the man returned some warmth to my bones.

Garrison stood over me, arms crossed. "You're still dressed."

Oh, right. That's what I was supposed to do.

Unable to explain myself, I just shrugged.

Even without words, understanding seemed to dawn on Garrison. He knelt on the floor, running one hand up my leg to settle on his knee.

"Want me to do it?"

"Yes." I closed my eyes and let my head knock against the wall. "I just... don't want to think right now."

A rare smirk spread across Garrison's face as his hands inched farther up my legs "I can help with that."

Taking control, he yanked both of our clothes free, tossing everything aside into a forgotten pile on the floor.

I let myself be manhandled, not even caring when I heard the sound of ripping fabric. Between each article of clothing removed, we stopped to kiss again. The pleasure of tangling tongues and warm lips distracted me to the point that I didn't even realize when all my clothing was gone.

My nakedness didn't register until strong hands suddenly flipped me around, so I knelt with my back to Garrison and my forearms braced against the wall.

"What are..." I never got to finish my question as Garrison gripped my hips and coaxed my legs apart. Two slicked fingers pressed inside me, breaching my hole and sending a thrill up my spine as my inner muscles were forced open.

Oh, that's why Garrison had disappeared. He'd been searching the bathroom for supplies, since neither of us had lube stored in our pockets.

Maybe I would have to start carrying some around, if this was going to be a repeat occurrence.

Fuck, I hoped it would.

I didn't know what I would do if Garrison chose to leave after this.

Warmth spread along my skin as Garrison draped over my back. "I can practically hear you thinking." The fingers inside me started moving, thrusting in and out while simultaneously scissoring open. "I'm going to have to up my game."

"Fuck, just... ah." Garrison's fingers hit a particularly sensitive spot and my legs trembled. "Just fuck me already."

"Hmm, no." Garrison struck the same spot again with deadly accuracy. "You said you don't want to think. Yet, you still seem coherent. No, I'm going to have to put in a lot more work."

A third finger joined the first two, straining the rim of my hole as it stretched to accommodate the new addition. All three fingers massaged against my prostate. The constant pressure on such a sensitive spot made me tremble and my forearms slid down the wall until I was nearly bent over.

An orgasm built under my skin shockingly fast. I moaned and curled my hands into fists, eager for the inevitable release.

Yet, before I could tip over that edge, Garrison suddenly stopped and pulled his fingers free. "Seems like you're ready."

I groaned in frustration and looked back over my shoulder. "I thought you were going to help me?"

"I am." Garrison grabbed something out of sight.

The sound of a crinkling wrapper had me twisting my spine to an uncomfortable angle to see what was happening. I watched as Garrison rolled a condom down over his cock and tried to ignore the feeling of disappointment that such a sight brought.

I wanted to feel Garrison inside me without any barrier between us. The demand to get rid of the condom was on the tip of my tongue, but I kept the words behind my teeth. Although I was certain that we had nothing to worry about— I'd snuck a look at Garrison's medical files and knew the man was clean—giving up such protection would require trust from both sides.

I was ready to trust. I already trusted Garrison with my life. Trusting the man with my health seemed like a step down in comparison.

But did Garrison trust me?

Probably not.

I'd lied to him, after all.

No, we would need to work up to that level of trust. So, for now, the barrier remained between us.

Condom in place and wrapper tossed aside, Garrison's hands returned to my hips.

I braced myself, expecting Garrison to push inside me just like he had with his fingers. Instead, I gasped in surprise when Garrison pulled me backward instead. My limbs flailed as I found myself sitting on Garrison's lap. His cock slotted between the globes of my ass.

Promising, but distinctly not what I wanted.

Letting out a high-pitched whine, I tipped my head back to rest on Garrison's shoulder. "Now you're just being mean."

One of Garrison's hands slid up my chest to rest lightly on my collarbone. "This is what you asked for." Garrison's breath heated the side of my neck. "You wanted me to take control. That means we go at my pace. So, relax and enjoy it."

He let our hips grind together, his cock slowly sliding against my hole without breaching inside.

That went on for several minutes. It was a slow kind of torture. So close to the fulfillment that I wanted, but never taking the last step. There were a few moments where it seemed like Garrison might be lining up to finally start fucking me properly. The head of his cock would press against my hole, just one thrust away from slipping inside. Yet, each time it would slide right past, and we would return to our slow grind.

My recently denied orgasm already left sparks dancing under my skin. The constant stimulation against my sensitive rim had me panting. I could barely get the words out as I begged.

"Please, come on. Hurry up. Garrison, just... fuck. I need you inside me already."

Warm lips pressed a line of kisses up my neck before Garrison spoke directly into my ear. "You really are a spoiled brat. Someone needs to teach you patience."

Despite his words, he finally gave in to my demands. Wrapping one arm around my waist, he held them tightly together as he finally thrust inside.

I moaned as Garrison's cock filled me much more than even three fingers had. My hands scrambled for purchase on the arm wrapped around me. I wanted to push back against Garrison, but our position didn't really allow much movement from me. All I could do was relax and submit to the invasion of my body.

This wasn't the first time we'd slept together. However, the position was new. Something about it made Garrison feel bigger than normal, and it seemed to take forever before the other man was buried all the way inside me. I felt completely split open, and pleasure ran over my skin like static. I expected Garrison to pull back out and start thrusting to really get us going, but the man stayed still.

A minute passed and nothing happened. We merely remained there, panting together until our breathing matched. I squirmed, trying to find more friction.

Garrison's arm tightened around my waist, keeping me from moving. "Stay still." His other hand ran down my stomach with a light, ticklish touch. "You're going to learn patience."

The voice speaking directly into my ear sounded serious. I knew Garrison's mind wouldn't be changed. My only choice was to obey. I tried to sit as still as possible as Garrison let go of my waist so both hands were free to wander. They ran up and down my body, toying with my nipples and caressing my thighs. With each touch, more pleasure sang through me and slowly pooled in my belly.

I jumped when Garrison's hands finally made contact with my weeping cock. The grip was light, fingers dancing over the shaft rather than gripping it firmly like I wanted. I gripped Garrison's hand, trying to coax the man to stroke me properly.

All I earned for my effort was a slap to my knuckles.

Message received.

I kept my hands out of the way by resting them on my own knees.

Although I couldn't see it, I could feel Garrison's grin as the man breathed praises against my ear.

"Good boy. Sit properly and take your lesson."

Garrison stroked my cock with such a light touch our skin barely made contact, while his other hand continued to explore the rest of my body.

All the while, I trembled as I forced myself to sit still while speared on the other man's impressive cock. My inner muscles seized around the hard shaft, desperate for more stimulation. I tipped my head back, exposing the long line of my throat, and counted my breaths. Each beat of my heart was a fight for control, and I was determined to win.

A sharp pinch on my thigh broke my concentration. My hips jerked, pushing Garrison's cock deeper inside me. It hit something sensitive, flooding me with a bright burst of ecstasy. I nearly came on the spot. One more touch would have been enough to send me over the edge.

Instead, Garrison removed his hands completely from my skin.

I whined a wordless protest as my body kept twitching with need, driving him deeper and deeper into me.

Garrison's voice was low and soothing when he spoke. "Calm down. I'm not done yet."

Only when I finally managed to regain control and sit still did Garrison's hands resume their attentions. He gripped my cock a little firmer this time, one finger toying with the barbell piercings along the underside of my shaft.

"I didn't get to explore these too much last time. How long have you had them?"

A minute passed before I realized Garrison had asked a question. "Four years."

Garrison pushed on the end of one of the barbells, causing the bar to slide back and forth under my skin. I bit my lip and tried to ignore the delicious ache it caused.

"I got the first one on a drunken dare, but then I liked it, so I went back for two more."

With his thumb, Garrison pressed down on the lowest piercing. The gentle touch created a delicious ache, like stretching a sore muscle. It was a mix of pleasure and pain that made me shiver.

Seemingly growing bored playing with only one piercing, Garrison shifted his grip to massage upward, letting his thumb ride the hills and valleys of each bar. "I've never thought about it before, but now I'm curious."

I shuddered and slumped forward. Only Garrison's arm around my chest kept me upright. "Curious?"

I was jerked backward so my back pressed flush to Garrison's chest. The man started stroking my cock in earnest, while also leaning in to nip at the junction of my neck and shoulder.

"Curious what these will feel like when you fuck me."

All at once, my stomach dropped into an endless abyss. Pleasure shot through me like lightning. My orgasm was sudden and strong, causing every joint in my body to lock up.

I couldn't even make a sound as I came. Just trembled as wave after wave of pleasure hit me all at once.

It wasn't just the shock of hearing a curse word fall from Garrison's lips, although that was also a surprise. No, what really pushed me over the edge was the insinuation that we'd be doing this again in the future.

Did this mean Garrison wasn't going to leave?

My climax finally ended. With a sigh, I slumped against Garrison, but the man didn't loosen his hold. As I regained my breath, I became acutely aware of the hard shaft still buried inside me and stretching me open.

I wasn't even surprised when Garrison gripped my hips and lifted me up a few inches only to immediately let go. I dropped back onto Garrison's lap, and his cock plunged back inside me.

"No, wait... I can't..." My words could barely be heard around my moaning. I may as well not have spoken at all as my pleas for mercy went unheeded. Strong hands kept a hold of me, bouncing me on Garrison's lap. Over and over, I was lifted and pulled back down, forcing Garrison's cock to slam right into my prostate each time.

I rode the line between pleasure and pain as nerves already overstimulated from my orgasm were repeatedly assaulted.

A line of spit dripped from the corner of my panting mouth, but I didn't even have enough strength to wipe it away. I was a ragdoll being ruthlessly fucked by my master.

Garrison seemed determined to make it last as long as possible. Each time the man neared his own end, he'd slow down. Then, after a moment to regain his composure, he'd speed up again with even more enthusiasm.

I wasn't sure how long it went on for. It felt as though I'd passed out, though I remained completely conscious. My own arousal slowly came to life again, bobbing between my legs in time with each thrust.

A voice in my head reminded me that my hands were free. I could take care of my own arousal if I wanted to. My fingers twitched with the desire to do so, but I couldn't find the strength to raise my arms.

One of Garrison's hands slid down and gripped my cock, giving the shaft a few hard strokes. That was all it took to push me over the edge again.

We came at the same time, trembling together as we rode out the last of our pleasure. I nearly face-planted into the floor the moment Garrison pulled out of me. I braced one trembling hand against the carpet to try and stay upright, but I could already tell it wouldn't last. Every muscle in my body seemed to have been replaced with Jello.

I didn't even have the strength to struggle when strong arms wrapped back around me, and I was lifted off the floor. Garrison carried me to the bed, where I was gently laid out over the mattress.

I closed my eyes and floated on a cloud of cotton and silk. I heard Garrison walk away but didn't bother to open my eyes. The only thing in that direction was the bathroom.

A minute later, Garrison returned with a wet washcloth.

The water was warm, but I still groaned in protest as Garrison cleaned us both up. The moment it was done, and the washcloth was gone, I pulled him into the bed with me. Hard muscles covered by soft skin made for much better bedding, and I cuddled against Garrison like I was getting ready to hibernate.

We lay together in silence for a while, both drifting on the edge of consciousness.

Judging by the clock, at least an hour passed before I felt capable of talking. Keeping my head pillowed on Garrison's chest, I looked up at him with curious eyes.

"It's probably too early to ask, but... Earlier you mentioned wanting to sleep together again. Was that just sex talk, or..."

Garrison took a deep breath, causing my head to rise and fall. He didn't answer right away. The weight of so many different words danced behind his eyes as he considered them one by one.

"It's true that I would like to know how

it feels to have you inside me. There are a lot of things I'd like to experience with you. Whether or not I get to know these things, however, is up to you."

I sat up so I could look Garrison directly in the eye. "Up to me? How so?"

Again, Garrison didn't respond right away. He stared at the ceiling, watching some far horizon only he could see.

"You asked me once about my tattoo."

Not sure what to say in the face of such a non sequitur, I merely nodded and waited for Garrison to continue.

"Each field cross represents a fellow soldier I saw die. A few happened over the years I served, but most were lost on my last mission."

The rest of the story lingered in the air between us, eager to be told. Yet, Garrison struggled with the words. He opened his mouth several times like he was about to start talking, but each time he would scowl then close it again.

Though I still didn't know what this had to do with his question, I figured a little prompting couldn't hurt.

"To lose so many people at once, I'm guessing something went wrong."

I had never counted the number of

field crosses on Garrison's tattoo, but there were enough to completely encircle the man's right bicep.

One of Garrison's hands tangled in the hair at the base of my neck. He toyed with the strands there, seemingly unaware that he'd turned me into his own personal fidget toy.

"I'm not sure if something went wrong, or if we just never had all the information in the first place. It was a standard mission. Intel said there were enemy combatants in the area, so we came prepared."

The hand in my hair stopped and lay still against the base of my neck. I didn't speak. I barely dared to breathe for fear of breaking the moment.

"We weren't prepared for child soldiers. There were five of them, pointing guns at us they could barely lift. The oldest one couldn't have been more than ten. If they were adults, I would have shot them on sight. But I wasn't prepared for kids. None of us were."

A hitch in Garrison's throat distorted his words. He coughed, trying to cover the emotional reaction, but at such close proximity I could see the lights dancing off repressed tears in Garrison's eyes.

I chose not to comment on any of it and instead pushed my head into Garrison's hand to encourage him to play with my hair again. The action made me feel like a cat begging to be petted. In the span of a few minutes, I'd gone from fidget toy to emotional support animal.

Yet, it worked. Garrison's voice returned to normal, and he was able to talk clearly again.

"I could tell from the looks on my comrade's faces that they wouldn't be able to do it. They couldn't kill children. I was the one in charge. It was my responsibility to protect my people. But I hesitated. One of the kids managed to pull the trigger and shot me in the knee. It set off a survival instinct in me. For that brief moment, I no longer saw children. All I saw were enemies. I killed all five of them."

I remembered the first time I'd had to kill someone. My father had set it up so that I could "get a taste for it". The gun had trembled so badly in my hand that I missed my original target. Luckily, it had still been a fatal shot so no one noticed how badly I'd messed up.

I'd been a teenager then. Practically a kid myself.

In the years since, I'd killed enough people that my hands no longer shook. Yet, I still couldn't imagine what it would be like to kill a child.

"At least you saved your people."

I cringed the moment the words left my mouth. I couldn't have been more insensitive if I just shrugged and said, "well, it could be worse."

Luckily, Garrison didn't seem to hear me, too caught up in his own memories.

"It was all so pointless in the end. Those kids weren't meant to be a real threat. Just delay us. With my knee shattered, I couldn't keep up, so I sent my people ahead. I should have realized it was a trap. About a minute later, a bomb went off. Since I was so far behind, I avoided the main blast radius. But the rest of my people…"

Briefly, with delicate fingers, I touched the edge of a particularly long burn scar that wrapped around Garrison's ribs. "That's where you got the scars on your back."

Garrison nodded, though his gaze never left the ceiling. "Close enough to feel the heat, but far enough away to avoid the worst of the blast. Though it did throw me across the street. A few of my people were also far enough away that the blast didn't immediately kill them. But that was worse. Instead of a quick death, they suffered for a few days until they died from their burns."

Sighing heavily, Garrison moved me off him. At first, I thought he was going to leave. Perhaps recounting such memories had been a way to explain why he couldn't accept my position in a mafia family.

However, Garrison didn't leave.

Instead, he rolled over on his side, so he and I lay face to face.

"I spent the last few days thinking about the things I've done in the past, and what I'm willing to do in the future. But, before I can give you an answer, I still have one question I need to ask."

"Anything." It was a simple response, but I meant it. There was nothing Garrison could ask right now that would be too invasive. How many people I'd killed in my life. How many laws I'd broken. The details of my family's business. It was all on the table.

Instead, Garrison only asked, "Why?"

It was so simple that I had to ask for clarification.

"Why did you hire me as your bodyguard? I'm sure your family already has plenty of muscle on the payroll, and hiding the truth from me only put you in danger since I didn't truly know what I was guarding you against. So, why take that chance?"

Even if I could have brought myself to lie to Garrison, I knew I'd never get away with it. The man was too perceptive. It was a wonder I'd managed to hide the truth about my family for so long, and that was mostly by avoiding direct lies as much as possible.

"Honestly, I didn't take the threat on my life seriously at first. My previous bodyguard got killed at the club, so I needed a new one anyway, and I was annoyed about having to take over for my father. I thought it would just be a temporary thing. You were attractive, and seemed interesting, so I thought you could keep me entertained. It was like a game. But then, things did get serious, and I actually was in danger. For the first time, I looked around and realized that none of the people around me were really *mine*. Everyone worked for my family, and I would inherit their loyalty from my father. Aside from Ghita, and maybe my mother, no one was loyal to me because I was Alex. They were only loyal to me because I was a Mariano."

I smiled and sat up, wrapping my arms around my knees as I looked down at Garrison. The only time I ever got to see the man from this angle was when we were in bed, both naked and vulnerable.

"Except for you. You had no idea about the Mariano name, but you protected me anyway. It made me feel safe. I don't remember the last time I truly felt safe around someone."

Garrison sat up as well. The softness of the mattress meant that it was impossible to sit without slouching a little. This put our eye lines at exactly the same height.

"I've realized that I'm not as bothered about the whole mafia thing as I probably should be. It was the lying that actually upset me more. I've killed people before. I've followed orders that would be a crime if they came from anyone other than the military. However, there is one line I will not cross. If I stay and continue to support and protect you... can you promise with absolute certainty that I'll never have to harm another child?"

I suspected that for Garrison to stay, we would have to find some sort of compromise. I'd worried about what Garrison would demand, and if the price for his loyalty would be too steep.

This was the easiest promise I'd ever made.

"I promise I will never ask you to harm a child in any way. I have no plans to ever involve children in my family's affairs again." I placed a hand on Garrison's knee, just above the edge of the brace. "And if, for some bizarre reason, such a thing is necessary, I promise I will find someone else to handle the job. That's not something you'll ever have to worry about."

At these words, Garrison released a heavy sigh and the stiff line of his shoulders relaxed. "Then I think we can make this work."

With an agreement reached, we lay back down on the mattress together with my head pillowed on Garrison's shoulder. The lights were turned off so only starlight was left to illuminate the room. The trees outside created mosaic patterns over the floor that spun with each gust of wind.

I watched the play of dark and light, breathing in the peaceful atmosphere. A deep knot in my chest finally relaxed, and I took what felt like my first proper breath in days.

Eyelids drifting closed, I was almost asleep when Garrison interrupted the silence.

"You know, we still need to figure out who's actually trying to kill you."

Oh, yeah. That was still a problem. I had been so distracted by not dying, I'd almost forgotten about the threat that started everything in the first place.

"You know, I might have an idea about that."

CHAPTER SEVENTEEN

Garrison

THE FUNERAL FOR Alex's father lasted three hours. It was a grand event, though not excessive, and I was surprised by how normal everything was. I'd attended plenty of funerals in my life—the field crosses tattooed around my arm could attest to that—and this one stood out only because of the number of people in attendance.

Less than a week had passed since Alex's kidnapping, and I was still on edge as I kept one eye on everything from the side of the chapel. Like most traditional catholic cathedrals, the building had been designed with aesthetic in mind more than safety. There were plenty of doorways and little hidden alcoves where someone could hide.

Plus, the distractingly ornate decorations didn't help. To me, it seemed like every praying statue and painted cherub was actually an enemy lurking in the shadows.

If I was still seeing a therapist, they would probably diagnose me with hypervigilance, but as far as I was concerned, there was no such thing as being too vigilant when someone was actually out to kill you.

Or kill Alex, which was basically the same thing.

Finally, with the afternoon sun creeping lower and lower through the stained-glass windows, the funeral came to an end. Some people left immediately, but all the Mariano family and everyone closely associated with them, were invited to a reception in the church's attached greenhouse. Small tables had been set up along the pathway to provide refreshments, encouraging guests to mingle among the flowers.

Alex posted himself under a large rose

trellis at the far end of the greenhouse, and I stood just a step behind.

We stayed there, finding camaraderie in silence as we watched over the reception. There were several people present who I recognized. Alex's uncle was a blight upon the crowd, while Ghita mingled easily. Meanwhile, Valente stayed off to the side in a similar position to a bodyguard. The man seemed motionless, but every now and then his gaze flickered over toward Alex.

Although, if one watched carefully, they would see Valente's gaze slip past Alex's shoulder to land on me, as if he couldn't quite process what he was seeing.

I was careful not to meet the man's gaze.

There were also several family members who I had never seen before but were easy to identify. Alex's mother shared a very similar bone structure with her son, especially when she was scowling.

Apparently, she didn't approve of the last-minute change to hold the reception in the greenhouse, but Alex had insisted.

However, there were still many more

people I didn't recognize. If I wanted to stay by Alex's side, I'd have to learn all their identities eventually, but for now, I treated everyone as a potential threat.

After the crowd had been allowed to socialize for a while, Alex stole everyone's attention by tapping one of his silver rings against the side of a champagne glass.

"Everyone. Thank you for coming. I'd like to say a few words."

What followed was the most standard speech I had ever heard. It didn't even specifically sound like it belonged at a funeral. Alex's speech could have just as easily been presented at a wedding, an award ceremony, or a court appearance, and it would have made equal sense.

Technically, nothing Alex said was insulting or untrue about his father, so no one had a reason to complain, but it was also obviously pointless.

A bit of excitement came when the greenhouses sprinklers suddenly turned on, watering the various plants and the guests as well. Everyone shouted, ducking under jackets and purses in an attempt to stay dry. The light spray raining down on them drifted through the air like mist, clinging to everything it touched.

Alex didn't even try to hide. He just stood under the falling water and laughed.

"Well, I guess that's my father's way of telling me to get on with it." The sprinklers shut off just as Alex raised his glass, toasting the sky as if it were a person.

Everyone followed him, though not everyone drank. Many were too suspicious to consume strange food or drink, even among their so-called family.

Considering what had happened to Alex, that was probably a good idea.

Alex took a quick sip of his own champagne, glancing toward me with a smirk, then set his glass aside.

"Now, I'm sure everyone is wondering what happens now. There has been some... confusion these last few weeks. Please rest assured, I am fully capable of taking over my father's position. In fact, I plan to start by reviewing all my father's previous dealings and plans in order to become better acquainted with the responsibilities expected of me." His expression twitched into a half-smile, and light glinted off the new silver ring in his eyebrow. "I assure you, no detail will go overlooked."

While the words sounded reassuring, a murmur of discontent passed over the crowd. Most people knew what Alex really meant.

No one was safe.

Not even those previously approved by David Russo. Any business that Alex didn't like would be dealt with accordingly.

Lorenz Mariano, Alex's uncle, looked especially upset, gripping his champagne glass so hard that the stem was in danger of breaking. I kept an especially close eye on the man and my fingers briefly twitched toward my gun.

However, Alex's uncle gave us no problems.

Instead, it was Valente who stepped forward from where he'd been hiding under the shade of a dogwood tree. His shoulders were stiff, as if his skeleton had been replaced with iron. It threw off his gait, so he didn't move with the same dangerous grace as usual.

"While we're all glad to hear that you're taking your role seriously, Alex. I think I speak for everyone when I say that a funeral is not an appropriate time for business."

A muscle in my jaw twitched as I ground my teeth together. Referring to Alex by his first name in such a formal setting, like he was addressing a child, was a blatant sign of disrespect. The man was too smart to have done such a thing by accident. He was intentionally trying to undermine Alex in front of all their family and allies.

"Oh, come now," Ghita interrupted, stepping up next to Valente. "Where else will he get a chance to address all of us? The family rarely gets together at the same time. I'm sure Uncle David would understand."

She slapped Valente on the shoulder in what looked like a friendly gesture, but the hit was unusually hard. Even from a distance, I could tell she'd put all the strength of her five-foot frame into that slap.

Valente shouted in surprise and staggered, grimacing as he clutched his shoulder.

My hand made contact with my gun. I was ready to charge forward, but Alex gestured for me to stay put.

With narrowed eyes, Alex left the frame of the rose trellis to stalk toward Valente with slow, measured steps.

"Something wrong, Valente? Are you injured?"

Before the man could answer, Alex grabbed the front of his shirt, popping off the buttons as he tore it open. There was a moment of struggle, but Alex managed to remove enough of Valente's jacket and shirt to reveal his shoulder wrapped in bandages.

Valente slapped Alex's hand away and pulled his clothing back into place.

"It's nothing. Just an accident."

"Oh, I agree." Alex tried to prod Valente's shoulder again, but the man dodged out of the way. "The gunmen at the aquarium didn't mean to shoot you. That's where it happened, right? When you were covering us so Garrison and I could escape?"

The rest of the greenhouse had gone so quiet, Alex and Valente may as well have been the only two people present. Even the plants seemed to be holding their breath.

As the pair stared each other down, I snuck a little closer, so I stood at Alex's back. From that angle, I couldn't see Alex's face, but the other man's tone of voice spoke volumes.

"When we questioned the survivors from that little shootout, they said they accidentally shot the man who hired them." Instead of the serious tone one would expect from a person accusing someone of betrayal, Alex spoke with a light tone of someone imparting a fun bit of gossip. "At first, I thought that was a lie meant to point us toward the Bianchi family, but then I realized something."

His sentence turned cold at the end, like stepping through a hole in the ice and falling into dark water below.

"My mother is good at what she does." He passed a nod to the woman in question standing just a few feet away. "She knows how to get a confession out of someone. She would never fall for a lie, so what the gunmen said must be true. They did accidentally shoot their employer, and it was not the Bianchi family. So, do you want to tell us, in your own words, where you got that bullet wound?"

Before anyone could move, Valente suddenly lunged, but he didn't aim for Alex. Instead, he grabbed Ghita, wrapping one arm around her throat from behind and pressing a gun to her head with the other hand.

Everyone around them jumped back. Many pulled out their own weapons, though they weren't sure where to aim.

I remained at Alex's side, my gun halfway out of its holster. Drawing it would be useless. I didn't trust my aim enough to shoot Valente without hitting Ghita.

Would a head on confrontation work better?

It might at least distract Valente enough to get the gun pointed away from Ghita.

No, Valente would likely just end up shooting Ghita before she could escape.

Despite the tense atmosphere, Valente's hands were steady as he pressed the gun a little harder into Ghita's temple.

"Accusing me of attacking this family. How did you come up with such an assumption?"

Rather than get upset, Alex turned his back on the entire situation and went over to the nearest table to pour himself another glass of champagne.

"You were surprisingly sloppy. Once I started thinking that it might be you, everything fell into place. You were at the aquarium, and you distracted my bodyguard right before someone took a shot at me, but you didn't try to protect me until it looked like I might survive. You're one of the few people who can get close enough to drug me and has enough authority to come and go as he pleases. You even helped interrogate the gunmen, where you could conveniently kill anyone who said too much."

Swirling the champagne in the glass, Alex watched the bubbles for a moment before he continued.

"When D'Angelo Bianchi also got shot, the opportunity to use him as a scapegoat was too perfect to ignore, wasn't it? Unfortunately, using a drug only the Bianchi family have access to, and burying me on their property was a little too obvious to be believed."

In the end, Alex put the glass down without taking a sip and turned back to face Valente. He smiled, and Valente's finger tightened on the trigger.

I wanted to smack Alex.

What was he doing, antagonizing the

man pointing a gun at his cousin's head?

"You've got no proof," Valente said, but even he didn't sound convinced. He knew this audience didn't require proof. The Mariano family lived by their own law.

Alex acted as if Valente hadn't said anything. "The one thing I can't figure out is why. Why try to kill me? Initially, I thought it was because you didn't want me to take over the family. But your first attempt on my life came before my father was dead. Before I even knew he'd been arrested. You've always been loyal to this family. So why?"

For the first time since I had met the man, Valente's hands shook. The barrel of the gun jerked against Ghita's temple, making her whimper, but she didn't flinch or try to pull away.

Valente's eyes turned to chips of flint, like hard bits of stone with no life inside. He calmed down by breathing deep through his nose.

"I wasn't loyal to the Mariano family. I was loyal to David. I've spent years as his shadow, and I was happy to do it because I thought that was where I belonged. A mafia king needs a wife and an heir to maintain power. He needs to be respected, and a relationship like ours... it wouldn't be respected." His hand faltered for a moment, dropping a few inches like he'd forgotten about the gun he was holding.

I crept forward, ready to yank Ghita out of the way, but before I could get close enough, Valente snapped back to attention.

"It was all fine, until you came along, refusing the respectable marriage arranged for you. Wearing your deviance like a badge of honor. And David just accepted it. He let you live the open life he never allowed for us."

While Valente ranted, Alex sighed and checked his watch. Once Valente fell silent, he finally looked up with an expression of bafflement written over his face.

"That's it? You set my father up to be killed, then tried to assassinate me, all because I'm gay and you're jealous?"

Pulling Ghita backward by the throat, Valente moved toward the door. "He was my life. I made him who he is, and I could take it away just as easily. He needed to be reminded of that."

People parted around out of his way as

he dragged Ghita across the greenhouse. She stumbled with each step, struggling to walk backward with an arm around her throat.

Yet, despite holding her hostage, Valente barely paid her any attention. His gaze remained firmly locked on Alex.

"At first, I was going to let you go, but you couldn't just fall into line. No, you started flaunting this outsider around, just to taunt me." Since both his hands were busy, Valente nodded at me.

If it was true that Valente and Alex's father were secretly lovers, then I could see how my presence would have exacerbated things. I stood beside Alex in the same way that Valente had stood beside Alex's father. The only difference was, we didn't have to keep our relationship secret.

Seeing someone else get exactly the life he wanted must have been like a slap in the face. He had reason to be upset, but that was no excuse for threatening Alex's life.

With a tired huff, Valente shook his head. "I'm not going to explain myself to a spoiled brat who had everything handed to him. You wouldn't understand. Now,

I'm leaving, and if you want Ghita to remain alive, then you won't try to follow me."

In response, Alex shrugged then looked down at his watch again. After studying it for a moment, he smiled.

"No, you aren't going anywhere."

Valente opened his mouth to argue, but when he did, an unexpected cough suddenly struck him. The violent hacking sound caused his whole chest to spasm, and a few drops of blood sprayed from his lips.

Ghita took the opportunity to flee. She pushed his arm off her throat and ran to duck behind Garrison for safety.

Not once did Valente try to get her back. He was too busy struggling to breathe.

At the same time, everyone else in the room started showing the same symptoms. All except for Ghita, Alex, and me, of course. We remained fine.

I breathed a sigh of relief and shoved my gun back into its holster. Our plan had worked.

"What?" Valente managed to sputter before being cut off by more bloody coughing.

Several others around the greenhouse mimicked the question.

Alex clapped his hands together once, like closing a book at the end of a story.

"Perfect timing. That turned out to be one of my better plans." He inspected the leaves of the rose trellis, turning them over to reveal brown spots already forming on green surfaces. "Though, I do regret that the plants will probably die."

Still coughing, Valente fell to his knees and clutched his chest. His eyes, however, drifted toward the ceiling. "The sprinklers."

"Yep." Alex abandoned the leaves to address the suffering crowd. "I have to thank you, Valente. Being drugged sucked, but it gave me the idea. Though I couldn't just slip it into the wine. Too many suspicious people in our family. I couldn't be sure everyone would drink, so I needed another delivery system. The greenhouse was a lucky find. Sorry, about the last minute change, Mother. I know you hate things like that."

He nodded toward her in a show of genuine remorse.

She glared at him, obviously more furious about being poisoned than having her schedule interrupted. One hand gripped her chest as she struggled to speak around a violent coughing fit.

"I can't believe you would..." She didn't bother to finish that sentence. Of course, Alex would go so far. He was a Mariano. They won by any means necessary.

"Don't worry," Alex called to the group that was rapidly growing sicker by the second. "I have an antidote, of course. It's right here." He pulled out a box that had been hidden behind the rose trellis. "There's enough for everyone." From the box he pulled out a small glass vial filled with liquid.

It was the same vial Ghita, Alex, and I had taken earlier to spare ourselves the effects of the poison.

Alex sloshed the liquid around for everyone to see. "You can have it once you've sworn your loyalty to the Mariano family's new leader. But, since you should already be loyal, that won't be a problem, right?"

With me on one side and Ghita on the other, Alex stood below the rose trellis as one by one each person got on their knees to take their unholy communion. In exchange for a vow of loyalty, they were given a lifesaving vial.

Alex's mother was the first to take the vow, and although she was still angry about being on the receiving end of such a trick, there was a light in her eyes that spoke of pride. She had raised her son to one day take charge, and he was living up to those expectations spectacularly.

Throughout it all, Valente was left on the floor. His coughing grew quieter, though blood continued to drip from his mouth, until eventually he went silent.

From that moment on, the man never made another sound. Not even his heart dared to beat.

CHAPTER EIGHTEEN

Garrison

BACK AT ALEX'S apartment, I stepped across the already familiar threshold with the confidence of someone coming home. It had been a hectic couple of days, dealing with the fallout of David Russo's funeral. Many people were furious that Alex would dare go so far as to drug his own family. A quick reminder that Valente had been a trusted ally of the family for decades usually shut them up.

Surely, if Valente could turn out to be a traitor, then drastic measures must be taken to ensure trust and loyalty. Or else the whole family structure might crumble.

As soon as he was back in his own apartment, Alex let out a huge sigh and collapsed on the couch.

"I can't believe that's finally over."

I followed until I was standing over the couch, staring down at Alex's prone form.

"Everything went better than I expected. When Valente grabbed Ghita, I thought we might be in trouble. I'm glad she managed to stay so calm."

Dark eyes looked up at me, bright as beetle shells. "She trusts me." Alex propped himself up on his elbows and tipped his head to the side so his shoulder-length hair fell dramatically over the side of his face. "Do you?"

"Do I trust you?" I repeated. I pretended to think for a moment, hemming and hawing over the question like it was a difficult math problem I couldn't possibly solve.

Alex slapped my leg, careful not to hit my bad knee. "Asshole."

Unable to help myself any longer, I joined Alex on the couch, kneeling over the other man and pinning his wrists to the cushions. "Yes. I trust you."

"Enough to stay?" One of Alex's legs wrapped around my hip. "Even though my life's not in danger anymore?"

I laughed and buried my face in Alex's neck to stifle the noise. "I doubt this is the last time someone is going to try and kill you. You have a bad habit of pissing people off." My laughter died down and I raised my head to look Alex in the eye, close enough to see flecks of green within the black. "But yes, I'll stay. So long as you keep your promise."

Alex's previous vow, that I would never have to harm another child, hung wordlessly between us.

Both of Alex's hands gripped the sides of my head and pulled me closer. "Of course." He pressed our lips together briefly. "And you have permission to smack me if I ever break that promise."

He kissed me again, deeper this time, and we stayed locked together for several minutes. It was a slow, gentle exchange, broken only when Alex suddenly flipped us over so I lay below him.

"All right, enough serious talk. I'm tired of being so boring."

"If you call poisoning a room full of your own relatives boring, I don't want to know what you call exciting."

But I already had an answer to that as

Alex started undoing the buttons of my shirt.

We quickly stripped off all our clothes, not in the mood for taking things slow. However, as I tried to reposition us, Alex shoved me back down onto the couch.

"Nope. You stay right there. It's my turn."

It was a large couch, but still not big enough to accommodate both Alex and I. One of my legs hung over the edge of the cushion to rest on the floor, and my head pressed against the couch's arm. Yet, I wouldn't trade my position for anything as Alex spread my legs and slithered between.

The other man even took a moment to press a kiss to the scar on my knee before rutting our hips together in a pleasant exchange of friction.

The arousal that built under my skin felt lighter and more playful than usual. Like champagne bubbles traveling through my veins.

I almost didn't realize what was happening until Alex was reaching down to press one slicked finger inside me. Only when I felt the breach of my body did it hit me. I couldn't remember the last time I took this position during sex. Due to my size, and general demeanor, people usually assumed I'd want to be in charge.

Yet, Alex didn't even hesitate before claiming ownership of my body. One finger was immediately followed by a second, and they worked together to probe and stretch me in a way that few people had ever been brave enough to do before.

To be on the receiving end of that confidence was enough to leave me moaning, even before Alex's fingers struck against my deepest pleasure spot.

The two feelings together had me digging my nails into the cushions to keep from coming on the spot.

"Ready so soon," Alex teased, though his fingers never stopped moving. "You must be eager."

Pulling his fingers out of me, Alex sat back on his ankles and just admired me for a moment.

I tried not to squirm at the feeling of being so closely observed. I was forty-two, damn it. Far too old to feel like a blushing virgin.

"Get on with it already."

Shaking his head and clicking his

tongue like a stern librarian, Alex ran one hand up my stomach, mapping the peaks and valleys of my muscles.

"Patience. Isn't that the lesson you taught me last time? But, I guess you have earned it. Saving my life so many times. You deserve a reward."

Alex's hand trailed back down until he found my cock, giving the shaft a few light strokes. The gesture obviously wasn't meant to achieve anything. It felt more like a greeting to get my attention.

Alex then held up a condom between two fingers, still sealed in the wrapper. He didn't even need to ask. A single raised eyebrow was more than enough to convey his question.

I considered it for a moment, truly weighing my options. If I insisted, I knew Alex would use the protection without complaint. Yet, I also knew that we were both clean. Alex had admitted to reading my medical records, and let me see his own as compensation. There really wouldn't be much risk. Certainly, no more risk than the bullets and backstabbing knives we faced every day.

Decision made, I grabbed the condom from Alex and tossed it aside.

Alex's eyes lit up, and he eagerly slicked his own bare cock with more lube. The silver barbell piercings darted between his fingers, and I shuddered as I imagined what they would feel like inside me.

Would they be cold, or would the metal be as warm as Alex's skin.

How hard would they feel?

Would they shift around with each movement?

Alex grabbed my undamaged leg just behind the knee and pushed it upward to open me up even more.

We'd barely lined up when, with one decisive thrust, the head of Alex's cock pushed its way inside my body.

I bit my lip to stifle my moans as I felt my sensitive muscles stretch. A mix of pleasure and pain raced up my spine and set my brain on fire.

Alex moaned and gripped harder onto my leg. "Fuck, you're tight. No one's fucked you in a while, have they, big guy?"

"No one's—" I gasped as Alex shoved in a little deeper. "No one's been brave enough to try."

Bracing his hands on my chest, Alex

leaned close enough for our lips to brush. "You're a hard beast to tame, is that it? Hmmm. Challenge accepted."

Another little thrust of his hips pushed him inside just far enough for me to feel the first piercing pressing against the rim of my hole. It was cooler than the temperature of Alex's skin, but not as cold and unyielding as I'd imagined.

"Ready?" Alex asked, carefully watching my face for any trace of discomfort.

Breathing deep, I nodded.

In one steady thrust, Alex pressed the rest of the way inside me. His piercings slipped inside my body one by one, each bringing a little zing of pleasure as they stretched me in new ways.

As soon as he was all the way in, Alex pulled out again, moving faster this time.

I yelped as the piercings dragged against my rim again, this time teetering on the edge between pleasure and pain.

The last piercing had barely left me before Alex plunged back inside. Our hips crashed together, and my vision whited out for a moment. When I came back to my senses, Alex was fucking me in earnest; all the way out, then all the way in, without even a moment to pause in between.

I was a writing mess on the couch. Alex's cock filled me so perfectly, and the unexpected stimulation of the piercings added a wild thrill. Reaching up, I tangled one hand in Alex's hair and dragged him down into a heated kiss.

We moaned into each other's mouths, unwilling to part as Alex picked up the pace. The whole apartment filled with the sounds of slapping skin and low moans.

I closed my eyes, listening to the music of our shared pleasure and reveling in the feeling of Alex's repeated invasion.

Higher and higher the sensation built, until I was trembling under Alex's hand, threatening to fall apart with the slightest touch.

A particularly hard thrust seemed to punch deep into my gut. My spine arched so drastically, I lifted Alex off the couch, and my fingers clawed at the cushions as I came. I trembled through the aftershocks that raced along my nerves, feeling my own pleasure spill hot and wet across my belly.

Alex pressed inside me a few more times before following me over that edge.

A sudden surge of warmth filled me and I held Alex as close as I could.

In that moment, if I could have melded us together, I would have.

Eventually, we relaxed enough to separate, but Alex didn't go far. He collapsed on top of me, limbs sprawling in every direction as he used my chest as a pillow.

"You know, almost dying was worth it if this is my reward."

I pinched Alex in a sensitive spot just under the ribs. "Don't joke about that."

Alex flinched but didn't remove himself from his position draped across me like a blanket. "What, it's the truth. Besides, what do I have to worry about when you're here to save me?"

Running a hand over Alex's head, I brushed a stray lock out of his face. "Yes, I'll be here, as long as you'll have me."

The smile that Alex gave me was not the sarcastic smirk or the over exaggerated cheer that the man usually presented to the world. No, this was a genuine expression filled with naked joy that Alex unfortunately didn't express very often.

"Great. Then you can start by letting

me have you again." He sat up and ground our hips together, obviously eager for round two even before he'd fully finished catching his breath.

I simply reclined back on the couch and ran my hands over whatever bit of Alex's skin I could reach.

"All right. I trust you."

As I looked up into Alex's eyes, I knew we were both thinking the same thing.

"*I trust you*" sounded a lot like "I love you."

Dear Reader,

Thank you for reading Courting Danger, the first book in the Ruthless Empire series. For more morally gray alpha men who live and die by family loyalties and honor, and will unalive anyone who touches their man, snag your copy of book two, Chasing Danger.

If you enjoyed this book, please return to the online retailer where you made your purchase and leave me a review. Your thoughts may just encourage other readers to try my books, and help me continue writing the bad boys we all love. Even a few words means the world to me.

~Love, Evie Riley

OTHER BOOKS BY EVIE

Federal Protection Agency
Mason
Rafe
Ryzen
Cooper
Noah
Damien
Sebastian
Gabe
Logan

Ruthless Empire
Courting Danger
Chasing Danger
Kissing Danger

Smokejumpers
Hawke
Cyrus
Jase
Gage
Jackson
Xavier

Jasper Springs
Cade
Dawson
Drew
Grayson
Riley
Mitch

From The Edge
Shattered
Runaway
Jaded
Rescue
Hidden
Tormented

Gray Vale Pack
His Fated Mate
His Wounded Warrior
His Healing Heart

ABOUT THE AUTHOR

Evie Riley is a prolific, neurodivergent author known for her captivating MM romance novels. She has gained a significant following and topped the LGBT+ action and adventure bestseller charts with her series.

Evie's writing style often explores dark and gritty themes where her men must overcome difficult obstacles in their search for love, but she has also ventured into sweeter small-town romances, incorporating tropes like enemies-to-lovers, friends-to-lovers, age-gap, and forced proximity. She is known for crafting engaging romantic suspense novels and has a knack for creating interconnected series worlds that keep readers invested.

EVIE RILEY

Interestingly, Ms. Riley has hinted at exploring new genres, such as Alien Omegaverse Romance, in the future.

Outside of writing, she enjoys spending time at the beach and has a quirky personality, described by her partner as ranging from cute to deadly, depending on her blood-chocolate levels.

Evie spends her nights writing bad boys in love, and her days wrangling the sweet boys she loves.

www.ingramcontent.com/pod-product-compliance
Lightning Source LLC
Chambersburg PA
CBHW071424200726
48294CB00002B/510